EXPLORING AZEROTH

THE EASTERN KINGDOMS

Unto Spymaster Mathias Shaw, for his diligent and ceaseless service to the crown of Stormwind, and to Captain Flynn Fairwind, for rendering much aid to the Alliance during the Fourth War, I, Anduin Llane Wrynn, king of Stormwind, hereby grant temporary leave. During this time, the spymaster and captain shall travel the length and breadth of our fair continent, the Eastern Kingdoms, in order to inventory certain powerful artifacts and ascertain they are safely secured. They shall also meet with the spymaster's various contacts and learn all they can about the state of our isle and its unique places. Travel through Horde territory, including the cities of Silvermoon and the ruins of Lordaeron, has been transiently granted by the esteemed Horde council. Spymaster Shaw and Captain Fairwind shall conduct themselves as temporary ambassadors to the Horde during these times. I wish them both to know that their efforts during this time will continue to benefit all members of our noble Alliance. Our openness to the Horde, and their acceptance of our request, could be instrumental in creating a world where days of war and suffering become so rare as to be the stuff of tall tales told to future generations.

As always, the coffers of the crown are open to the spymaster so he may procure transportation and supplies for his lengthy journey. He and Captain Fairwind shall present this letter to the proper individuals and make their requests of them.

May the Light be with you, Spymaster, and you also, Captain. Rest assured the faith of this kingdom—and its king—certainly is.

Done this day, by my hand,

Anduin Llane Wrynn,

king of Stormwind

I WON'T LET YOU DOWN, MATE!

To all members of the Horde:

This letter grants the bearer and his companion safe passage through Horde territories. The Horde council is aware and approves of their business in our lands. If they are harmed or their free movement challenged in any way, we will exact justice.

High Chieftain

Baine Bloodhoof

EXPLORING AZEROTH

THE EASTERN KINGDOMS

CHRISTIE GOLDEN

BLIZZARD
ENTERTAINMENT

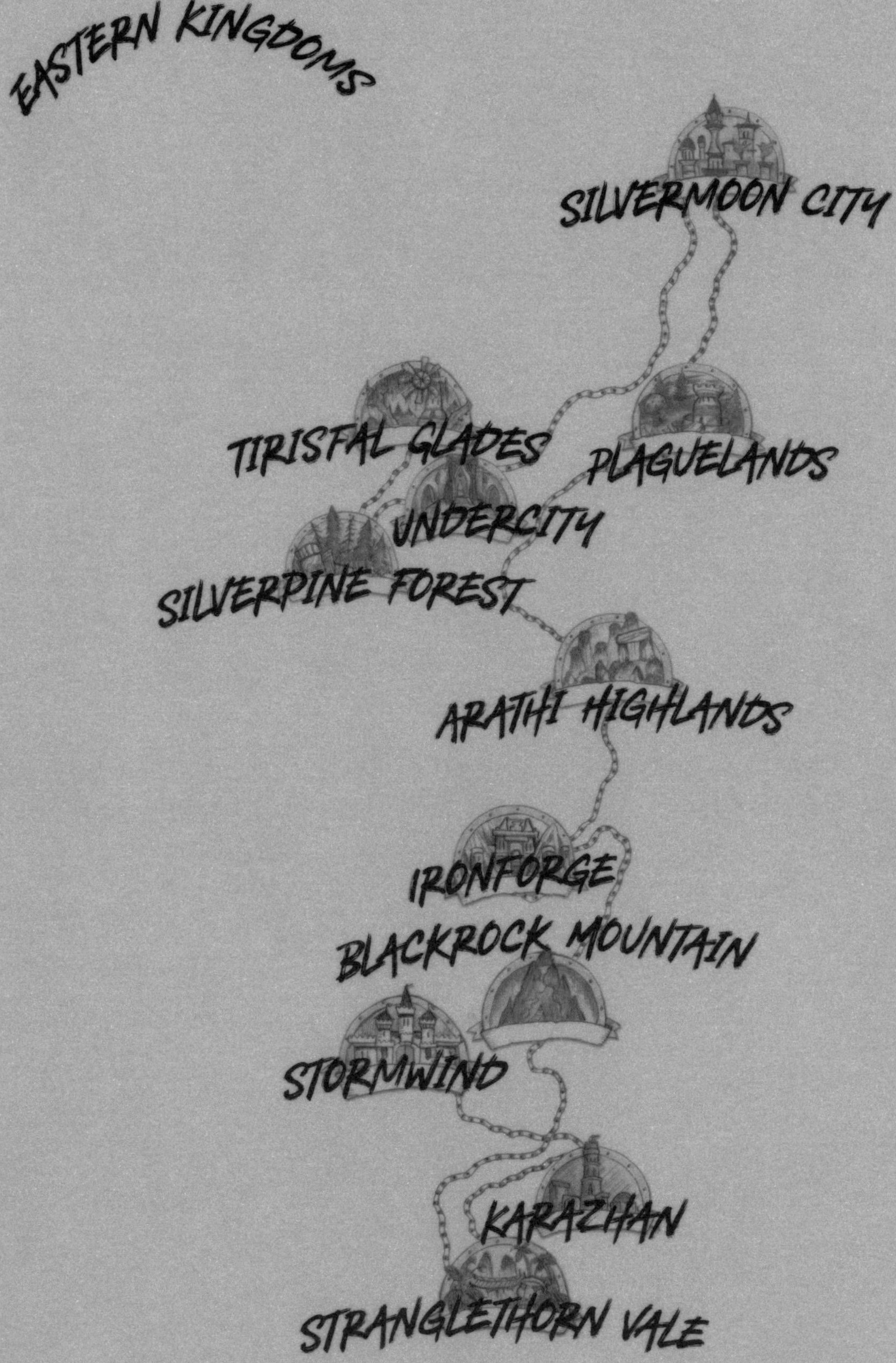

EASTERN KINGDOMS

SILVERMOON CITY

TIRISFAL GLADES

PLAGUELANDS

UNDERCITY

SILVERPINE FOREST

ARATHI HIGHLANDS

IRONFORGE

BLACKROCK MOUNTAIN

STORMWIND

KARAZHAN

STRANGLETHORN VALE

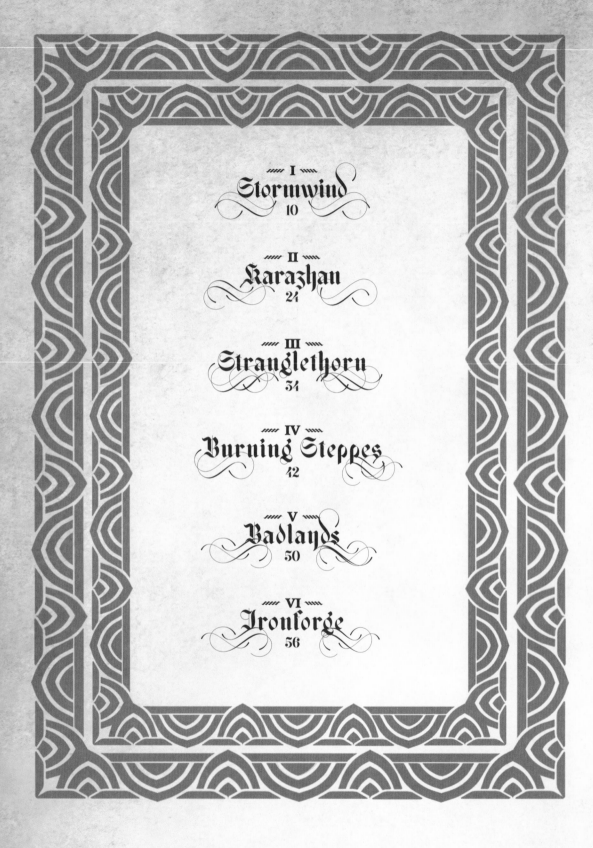

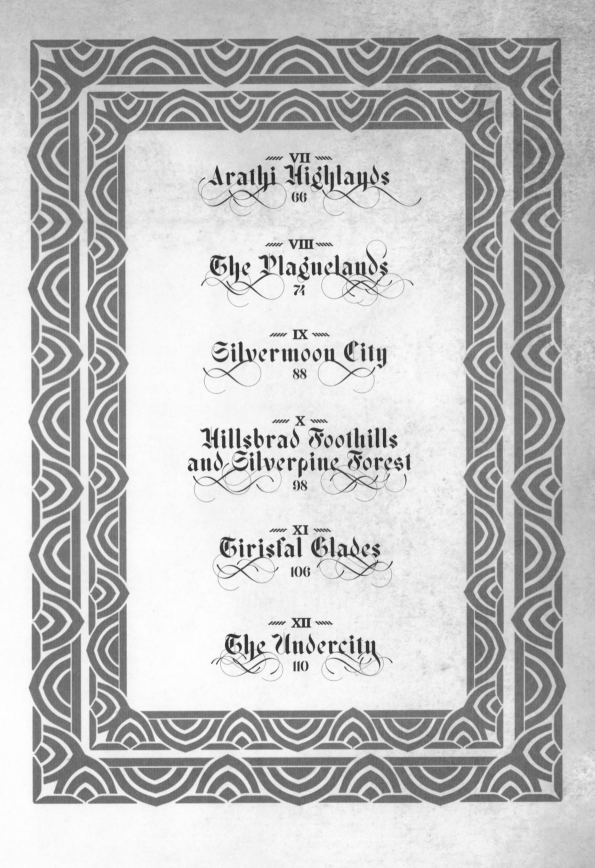

I

Stormwind

The city of Stormwind is the base of SI:7 operations. My agents know every inch of this place, and we have a few "friends" in nearly every quarter, selling goods, listening to strangers chat, and keeping an eye out on our behalf. The entrance to Stormwind itself is impressive: The bridge to the city proper is lined with large statues commemorating the fallen leaders of the Alliance expedition to Draenor. Fate itself was challenged and overturned as all five—Falstad Wildhammer, Danath Trollbane, Archmage Khadgar, Alleria Windrunner, and High Exarch Turalyon—turned out to be very much alive, though Alleria and Turalyon returned to us forever changed.

Stormwind is the beating heart of the Alliance and a major part of Azeroth's history. Established well over a thousand years ago, it's also seen its share of violence. In years past, the black dragon Deathwing destroyed vast sections of the city, but Stormwind experienced its greatest damage during the First War. The orcs forced a mass exodus to Lordaeron after occupying and devastating our city. A young Prince Varian was among the refugees' number, but eventually Stormwind was reclaimed and rebuilt by the Stonemason's Guild. They restored Stormwind to its former majesty, and their skill and distinctive style is evident in the keep and in the Cathedral of Light. And, while the different roofing material distinguishes each of the districts, nearly all exteriors in Stormwind are made from this white stone.

Unfortunately, what began as the stonemasons' rightful request for payment turned into a heated dispute between them and the nobles, who were urged on by Lady Katrana Prestor. Soon, things turned violent. Queen Tiffin was killed while she was attempting to calm the rioting stonemasons. Varian, enraged and grief stricken, came down hard on the rioters, who fled to Westfall. There, the once-respected guildmaster Edwin VanCleef stepped in to unite the angry stonemasons, using his training in the arts of stealth and subterfuge to form the Defias Brotherhood. Her Majesty's untimely death and the rise of the Defias remain a stain upon SI:7. Had we been able to determine that "Lady Prestor" was in reality the black dragon daughter of Deathwing and take out VanCleef sooner, so much tragedy could have been averted. Fortunately, the threat both she and the Defias posed has been neutralized.

Stormwind Keep

From its massive turrets, all of Stormwind City may be surveyed. For a king, this is essential for both studying the masses and as a strong reminder of what they must fight for. For a spy, any high place is a useful place. The Wrynn line has always welcomed the public into the keep . . . a decision that I still believe to be dangerous. Anyone is admitted not just to the petitioner's chamber but also the throne room and, on occasion, the War Room. Citizens make good use of the garden and the royal library, strolling the grounds and reading. There are of course several private areas—His Majesty's rooms, guest quarters for prominent visitors, even a small royal armory for extremely rare pieces. The keep also contains not just fiercely devoted guards but also a considerable number of agents at any given time, posing as lesser noblemen or servants to the crown. Varian and Anduin were and are aware of only a handful of them. There are also multiple secret passages through which the king might escape if need be. They are supposed to be unknown to anyone save us until needed. The young King Anduin, however, needed no secret passage; he managed to elude his guards with surprising skill. I was almost proud. He was found in the Gilded Rose tavern dressed as a commoner. Luckily, we were able to retrieve him before anything happened.

The Throne Room

Where Stormwind kings are crowned—and, once, murdered. King Llane Wrynn was assassinated here by Garona Halforcen.✶ The late King Varian and now King Anduin hold audiences in this chamber. Here as well, Onyxia's disguise as Lady Katrana Prestor was finally revealed, and here a good friend, Reginald Windsor, died protecting a young Prince Anduin. The gold and stained-glass throne that the line of Wrynn sits upon both inspires and intimidates. Which, I suppose, is its intended purpose.

✶ *Spymaster's Update: We have since learned that Garona's mind was not her own at the time of Llane's assassination. She has earned membership and good standing with the Uncrowned.*

I UNDERSTAND YOU HAVE TO WORK WITH WHAT YOU'VE GOT, BUT I'M SO MUCH BETTER THAN A KING-KILLER.

The War Room and Royal Library

The War Room's function is self-explanatory. It houses an enormous table map with movable figurines to allow the king and his generals to plan attacks, defenses, and other maneuvers. I have attended more than my share of meetings here, while serving two kings. Weapons line the walls, some for dignified display. Others simply rest here when not in use by His Majesty, including **Shalamayne**, the weapon wielded by first Varian and then his son; a single sword forged with two blades out of legend. **Fearbreaker**, the mace given to King Anduin by Magni Bronzebeard, also resided here for a time. During N'Zoth's incursion, Magni Bronzebeard requested the mace be returned to him to fight the corrupt Old God.

Directly opposite the War Room is a small, quiet garden. It's open to the air and therefore highly unsafe. I've spoken to Varian and Anduin both about taking precautions, but neither paid attention to my concerns.

Next to the garden is the Royal Library. A seldom-read book is a convenient place to stash a note, and many of the tomes provide useful research as well. Occasionally an older history book will reveal interesting tidbits (maps for forgotten areas, passageways sealed over but possible to render functional), which I will stash away for later use. Open to the public, the library offers a treasure trove of books such as *Beyond the Dark Portal, Civil War in the Plaguelands, Aftermath of the Second War,* and *The Alliance of Lordaeron.*

Once the library boasted a gallery featuring fine art and statuary, including figures of Mara Fordragon, King Llane, and Daelin Proudmoore. After Deathwing's attack, much of this chamber was damaged, and many of the works could not be restored.

p. 2

Beyond the Dark Portal

Convinced that Ner'zhul was planning a new offensive against the Alliance, King Terenas of Lordaeron sent his armies into Draenor to end the orcish threat once and for all. Led by Khadgar and General Turalyon, the Alliance forces clashed with the orcs across the burning landscape. Even with the aid of the elven ranger Alleria, the dwarf Kurdran, and the veteran soldier Danath, Khadgar was unable to prevent Ner'zhul from opening his portals to other worlds.

Aftermath of the Second War

There was nothing left for the ragged, scattered orc survivors but to flee to the last standing bastion of orcish power—the Dark Portal.

Turalyon and his warriors chased the remaining orcs through the festering Swamp of Sorrows and into the corrupted Blasted Lands, where the Dark Portal stood. There, at the foot of the colossal portal, the broken Horde and the rugged Alliance clashed in what would be the last, bloodiest battle of the Second War.

The New Horde

During his travels, Thrall found the aged warchief, Orgrim Doomhammer, who had been living as a hermit for many years. Doomhammer, who had been a close friend of Thrall's father, decided to follow the young, visionary orc and help him free the captive clans.

Supported by many of the veteran chieftains, Thrall ultimately succeeded in revitalizing the Horde and giving his people a new spiritual identity.

I HEARD HOW HE DIED. QUITE BRAVE, HONESTLY.

Lion's Rest

Lion's Rest is a quiet spot for reflection, memorializing the late King Varian Wrynn and all others who fell defending the Alliance in wartime. The tomb does not house the king's body, as it was not recoverable. The inscription reads:

> THE SON OF STORMWIND LIES HERE. BROKEN IN TWO BY HIS WEAKNESS, HE LIVED BY THE SWORD. FORGED TOGETHER AGAIN, THE GREATEST KING THE KINGDOMS OF LORDAERON HAVE EVER SEEN. HE LED THE MIGHT OF THE ALLIANCE WITH PRIDE. HE LIVES FOREVER IN OUR HEAVY HEARTS. REST IN PEACE, O SON OF STORMWIND.

Anduin often speaks to his people from here on solemn occasions. Nearby, there is a gate that leads into the sewers, and from there directly into the Stockades.

*I HAD NO IDEA!
SOUNDS LIKE THE IDEAL ESCAPE ROUTE FOR SOMEONE RUNNING RUM . . .
AND THAT SOMEONE DEFINITELY ISN'T ME.*

Cathedral of Light

Holy to all followers of the Light and priests and paladins far and wide, the Cathedral of Light continues to draw worshippers and penance seekers from across the Eastern Kingdoms. My agents and I favor the shadows the massive building casts, but even we can appreciate the serene environment the cobalt-inlaid stone halls create. Citizens often congregate in the Square for conversation and the occasional swiped apple. A great statue of Uther the Lightbringer tops the square's fountain with an inscription that reads:

> UTHER THE LIGHTBRINGER. A RIGHTEOUS PALADIN, AN HONORABLE MAN, AND A DEAR FRIEND. YOU WILL NEVER BE FORGOTTEN, BROTHER.

Many pause here to pay their respects. The Cathedral itself is an elegant and peaceful place for prayer and reflection, but not without some dark memories. Arthas Menethil was inducted into the Order of the Silver Hand here; many of those present later noted that the Light itself seemed uncertain whether to bless the young prince. And, for too long a time, Archbishop Benedictus—revealed to be the Twilight Prophet, leader of a doomsday cult—was in charge. The bell tolls the hour, and in times of danger it is rung to alert the populace. Its history is intriguing, in that it is a twin to Lordaeron's bell. Both were cast in the Great Forge in Ironforge as gifts of goodwill from the dwarves to their human allies. Its tolling once was a frequent reminder of friendship. Now, it recalls Lordaeron's fall with each resonant tone.

Armor Aside: *LAWBRINGER ARMOR*

Only paladins of impeccable commitment do not shrug beneath the weight of the Lawbringer armor. Adorned with golden wings and polished plates, these venerable armaments command attention. Senior paladins claim that the Light itself shines through the hallowed metal, calling favor down upon the wearer.

Catacombs

Beneath the Cathedral of Light are the catacombs of the honored dead—priests, war heroes, and paladins, among others. The living stayed here too, during the First War, hiding in safety as the orcs razed the city above. This is also a collection of drop points, usually in the alcoves themselves, as they are not likely to be frequently disturbed.

ACCORDING TO MATHIAS, A DROP POINT IS "A PLACE TO LEAVE A MESSAGE OR AN OBJECT. BEHIND A LOOSE BRICK, IN A CRACK IN A WALL, UNDER A CLAVICLE, THAT SORT OF THING." GHASTLY. TRULY GHASTLY.

Stormwind Cemetery

The nearby cemetery is a beautiful and peaceful place during the day. At night it is excellent for meetings and covert exchanges. Queen Tiffin's grave is here with this inscription:

> TIFFIN ELLERIAN WRYNN, QUEEN OF STORMWIND. FAIR AND JUST, A WIT AS QUICK AS HER SMILE. MAY THE LIGHT INHERIT YOUR WARMTH, FOR OUR WORLD GROWS COLD IN YOUR ABSENCE.

The epitaph was written by Varian. He was a difficult king to serve, but he was remarkable. The grief of losing Tiffin nearly crushed him: another moment where he learned patience from his young son. Well, now king and queen are together, or at least so High Priestess Laurena tells us.

Harbor

Stormwind's harbor is both pleasant and practical. Ships from nearly every Alliance territory used to dock here with regularity. However, with the events of the Fourth War, the exquisite vessels crafted by the kaldorei have been replaced with the less beautiful, but no less seaworthy, ships from our old friends, the Kul Tirans. Our newest dockmaster, Aron Kyleson, tends to the *Relentless*, which bears diplomats to and from Kul Tiras. Farther down the harbor, the dwarf Thargold Ironwing does good work for us. His gryphons supposedly carry tourists on sightseeing trips over the harbor, but he uses this cover to keep an eye out for anything that could be useful to SI:7. The lighthouse on a small island nearby has sat empty for some time. The harbor has been expanded in recent years and is much safer to enter than in the past. There's a tombstone nearby, likely the resting place of a long-ago keeper, but time has faded the inscription. A lower priority and a task for another day.

I WANT TO RIDE A GRYPHON!

Westfall

Westfall never quite seems to catch its breath. It was once green and fertile farmland but hasn't been so for a long time. The transients who arrived here after the Cataclysm continue to come and go, this time unsettled by a massive war, not a world's breaking. If there is any silver lining, they provide a rich source of rumors for SI:7 to investigate. The area was once lousy with members of the Defias Brotherhood; they may have been Stormwind's stonemasons, but they retreated here, making the labyrinth of caves beneath the town of Moonbrook their stronghold. Marshal Gryan Stoutmantle of Sentinel Hill hired a group of adventurers to defeat VanCleef. With support from Stoutmantle's soldiers, these heroes finally put an end to Edwin VanCleef. Things were quiet until VanCleef's daughter, Vanessa, returned to lead the organization for a time. No one—not even I—knew of her existence before then; as a child, she witnessed Edwin's decapitation from a hiding place on Captain Greenskin's pirate ship. The Defias followed her loyally, up to and including the burning of Sentinel Hill. Like her father, she fought to the end.✱

Sentinel Hill

Mindful of the severity of the Defias Brotherhood attacks in the past, Sentinel Hill is being rebuilt to eventually be larger and better fortified under Stoutmantle's watchful eye. The Westfall Brigade cooperates with us, managing the troublemakers as best they can and keeping at bay the foul gnolls, a threat that never seems to go away. They are slightly less well-organized these days due to the defeat of their leader, a large, surprisingly crafty brute called Hogger. He was a dangerous creature and we are well rid of him. Why the guards keep **Hogger's Trousers** as some sort of memento in the Stormwind stockades is beyond me, but if it harmlessly improves morale, so be it.

The tower on Sentinel Hill is also where weapons donated by champions of the Alliance are safely kept. Here on display are the sword, axe, and hammer wielded by the tauren first mate of Greenskin's ship, Mr. Smite. He liked to toy with his victims, letting them think they could win while he gradually wielded more and deadlier weapons. His fellow shipmate, the murloc chef nicknamed "Cookie," also has a weapon mounted here. It's called **Cookie's Tenderizer**, and it's a rolling pin. Amusing, until you realize how many skulls he shattered with it. The final piece on display is the **Cruel Barb**, the very weapon Edwin VanCleef wielded as he died. I hear he put up a good fight.

WORD HAS IT YOU KNEW HIM. IS THAT WHY YOU WENT TO THAT OLD MINE?

✱ *Spymaster's Update: Vanessa VanCleef survived, and after an honorable duel for the position, is now a member in good standing with the Uncrowned.*

II
Karazhan

uilt upon a ley line nexus hundreds of years ago, the tower of Karazhan is now forever associated with its darkest son, the last Guardian of Tirisfal—Magus Medivh. His worst crime against our world: conspiring with Gul'dan and opening the Dark Portal. He was possessed by the Leader of the Burning Legion, Sargeras, even before his birth, so Medivh didn't stand a chance. He, along with his mother, Aegwynn, and his faithful steward Moroes, were buried nearby in the small graveyard known as Morgan's Plot. Few are improved by death, but Medivh's spirit was one. His shade regretted what he had done while living, and he was key to saving Azeroth during the Third War.

Some of the world's most powerful—and dangerous—artifacts are secreted here. A wise spymaster always wants to know where objects of such significance are safely locked away.✱ One reason there are so many important relics stored here is because Medivh once cursed beings now known as the Dark Riders to scour the world collecting artifacts for him. These were unfortunate merchants in life with whom Medivh was displeased. As a way to spend eternity, traveling Azeroth for interesting and powerful artifacts isn't as bad as some fates I could think of.

The place is vast, the ghosts a multitude, and danger everywhere. Best to enter through the servants' quarters. In the stables, Attumen the Huntsman once terrorized interlopers. He rode a magnificent mare named **Midnight**, who fought her master's enemies along with him. Local tales tell of an unnatural steed who still roams the grounds, seeking a worthy rider.

> ✱*Spymaster's Update: This particular task has been much eased since Khadgar moved into Karazhan. He's withstood the temptation of this place before; I feel comfortable knowing he is here. Of course, it never hurts to be careful. We usually check up on him, too.*

Banquet Hall and Grand Ballroom

Ghosts are quite literally everywhere here—dancing, flirting with one another, and being annoyingly arrogant. With lives like that, maybe it's best they're spirits now. Medivh threw notoriously decadent parties, often with prominent guests invited to share a meal with the master of Karazhan. All six of the nobles of Darkshire were the final ones to enjoy such hospitality as living beings; that night, Medivh, driven insane by the demon within, attempted to slaughter all who attended. The unfortunate steward's mind was never the same after that night. Despite surviving the horrible event, he was later to die at the hands of his master regardless. Earlier, I said Moroes was buried at Morgan's Plot. He was—until Medivh raised him as an undead creature as mad as his master was. He's really the only one I have pity for. A word of warning: A traveler passing through may see the ghosts of Anduin Lothar, King Llane Wrynn, and a sleeping Medivh. I've never had trouble personally, but they should still be treated with caution.

Opera Hall

Those who survive report that the performances are often unnaturally magnificent, but it seems to depend on which play the spirits were inclined to perform. Some, especially the histories, were riveting; other stories centered around magical realms and ill-fated romances, providing fascinating insight into the places and people that inspired them. Being the unstable place that Karazhan is, our current intel shows that new plays continue to manifest. I suppose the dead have all of eternity to perfect their repertoire.

PLAYS ARE A GRAND WAY TO PASS TIME WHEN YOU'RE AT SEA. IT MIGHT SURPRISE YOU, MATHIAS. BUT I'M A MAGNIFICENT THESPIAN.

Nightbane

The monstrous Nightbane was once the blue dragon Arcanagos. Slain by Medivh and raised by Violet Eye's adventurers, the bones of this once-noble creature are now imbued with fiery wrath. The last agents I sent to speak to Medivh's shade said the hulking mass of reanimated dragon bones appeared just after engaging—or at least, so says their scorched intelligence report. As skeletons and flame alike obey Nightbane's command, to watch one's step would be an understatement.

THE WHAT OF WHAT, NOW?

The Maiden of Virtue

Medivh's parties—and other activities—were so depraved that they drew the attention of the titan keeper we know as The Maiden of Virtue. She made her way to Karazhan in an attempt to purify this place of all its immorality. Clearly, she failed. She remains still as the stone that comprises her until her attention is drawn by someone she thinks is either Medivh—or as debauched as he was. Her judgment seems to have decayed over time, because with enough provocation, she will attack anyone regardless of their moral character. Some of the objects found in her vicinity seem incongruent with her name, such as the **Vest of Wanton Deeds**, a barbed **Choker of Discipline**, and a pair of manacles. I suspect these are likely things she confiscated from her victims. It is wise not to anger her, for she will pursue you without tiring until either you subdue her, or she does the same to you.

The Menagerie

The arcane guardian dubbed the Curator continues to reactivate from time to time. If he is, and you need to infiltrate the area behind him, he will do everything to prevent you from trespassing. Not only is he quite massive, that lumbering gait is deceptively fast, and the Curator is extremely strong. Even alone he's a formidable enemy, but he is also able to call forth smaller, spark-like creatures to fight alongside him. He was designed to protect the secrets of this place: things that were dangerous, magical, beautiful, and often unique. Over the years, these treasures were broken or lost, yet he is fierce in his duty even now.

Khadgar

Understanding Khadgar is . . . complicated. He was once Medivh's apprentice, but when Medivh fell under Sargeras's control, Khadgar, a mere youth, stood beside Anduin Lothar to stop his old master. During that fight, Medivh attacked Khadgar by draining his life force, prematurely aging his once-young pupil. Even so, Khadgar was able to plunge a sword into Medivh's heart. Although his body was old and fragile, Khadgar's mind remained that of a teenager. He continued to fight alongside Azeroth's greatest heroes, even venturing through the Dark Portal. He led the combined forces of the Horde and Alliance not once, but twice—once against the Iron Horde and again against the Burning Legion. Somehow, between when he stepped through the Dark Portal and when he returned, his appearance seems much younger. I hear that when pressed about it, he smiles but never responds. Young, old, or in-between, he is an extraordinary man in almost all respects. After the defeat of the Burning Legion, a powerful display of cooperation between the Horde and Alliance, the archmage was, understandably, disappointed we could not keep that unity.✷ He refused to participate in another war between Azeroth's people and retreated here, hoping to aid our wounded world by finding a solution in one of Karazhan's many ancient tomes.

✷ *Spymaster's Update: Horde and Alliance have recently signed an armistice agreement. Varian loved a fight, and he died in one. Anduin is of a different nature, be it bold, naïve, or something in-between. As for myself, I have yet to find my place in all of this. My position is one of distrust and suspicion by nature and training.*

Spymaster Shaw,

It is always a pleasure to see you, and your new friend Captain Fairwind is most entertaining. I appreciate that you have made no attempt to persuade me to resume my public duties. The recent armistice has given me a faint glimmer of hope that, one day, the children of Azeroth will realize that more unites them than divides them, but I temper such expectations.

Here is the report I've prepared for you regarding the status of our current artifacts. They continue to be stored in the no-longer secret trophy room in the Menagerie area. Our old friend the Curator continues to decline, though I am attempting to repair him. For the time being, he is still erratic.

Safe journeys,
Khadgar

TOUCH YOUR COLLAR, MATE, OR YOU'LL JINX IT!

INVENTORY OF MAJOR ARTIFACTS
HELD AT KARAZHAN

The CLOAK OF PURITY protects its wearer from corrupting influences and allows them to see through illusions. Revil Kost, one of the angriest priests I've ever met, returned it here after availing himself of its protection as he hunted the Dark Riders. THE STAFF OF INFINITE MYSTERIES may be ostentatiously named, but it is indeed mysteriously beautiful and quite powerful. I've found it to make the mind sharper and less weary. It used to belong to the Curator, but I think it's much safer tucked away here. He doesn't seem to miss it. I also have here a pair of the astonishingly scarlet, some might even say "ruby," slippers that one of the opera singers wore. Old as they are, they're still quite lovely and still quite functional. They will magically return you to a designated location.

Formerly stored in the catacombs was the scythe known as ULTHALESH, THE DEADWIND HARVESTER. It deserves mention as it contains the souls of demons who rebelled against Sargeras. It's one of the few things said to strike fear into the Mad Titan's black heart. The scythe is, I believe, now in the hands of a trusted champion of the Black Harvest, and I dare say Ulthalesh still hopes one day to slay Sargeras.

And lastly, a humble thing. It is a signet ring that belongs to Garona; I believe she lost it while she was here years ago. Would you return it to her, please?

III
Stranglethorn

The southernmost part of the Eastern Kingdoms is Stranglethorn, noteworthy for three things:

1. Jungles: All agents must be equipped with an emergency pouch containing the antidotes to . . . well, everything. The Explorers' League has a dig site here, and the big-game hunters Hemet Nesingwary Senior and Junior have left their mark past and present. Hemet Nesingwary Sr. is noted for his book *The Green Hills of Stranglethorn*. It's an account of his adventures hunting some of the beasts in this area. I've read it twice myself, and a few lines have stayed with me that describe some of the game animals quite vividly:

ON A ROCKY PRECIPICE ABOVE, SILHOUETTED BY THE SETTING SUN, I COULD MAKE OUT THE LARGEST CAT OF PREY I HAVE EVER LAID EYES UPON. I WAS ABLE TO LOOSE ONE CLUMSY VOLLEY WITH MY RIFLE, BUT THE CAT HELD HIS GROUND. HE GROWLED ONCE AGAIN, THIS TIME LOUDER THAN THE FIRST, AND VANISHED.

2. Trolls: Stranglethorn Vale was the center of the Gurubashi Empire, which at its height ruled over lands from Stranglethorn Vale to the Echo Isles. They are scarcer there than they were in their glory days, but they still hunt their ancestors' lands. Trolls have long memories and remarkable skill in close combat.

3. Pirates: The place is crawling with the unsavory pests, chief among them the Bloodsail Buccaneers. Only seaworthy agents are sent here, but we do rely on Booty Bay gossip for helpful information. A bilge rat can be persuaded with the right kind of cheese.

HOME AT LAST!

Zul'Gurub

The former capital of the Gurubashi Empire, Zul'Gurub remains an extraordinarily dangerous place. The local trolls are brutal, violent, and swift. The loa Hakkar the Soulflayer introduced the trolls to blood magic here, over a thousand years ago, and his proclivities remain strong in his followers.

Many venture into this ancient city in search of priceless treasure and artifacts. To be sure, some emerge victorious, but most don't emerge at all. Between the perils of the jungle and Hakkar's lingering influence, agents should avoid Zul'Gurub unless specifically directed to investigate.

I LIKE WHERE THIS IS GOING.

Armor Aside: *BATTLEGEAR OF MIGHT*

Within the chest of each warrior beats a noble heart—and that heart needs protection from a lucky arrow or quick jab with a blade. The Battlegear of Might provides heavy defenses for such fighters and a mighty silhouette to boot. Its wearers are known to channel their rage into devastating blows and defeat their enemies without earning so much as a scratch.

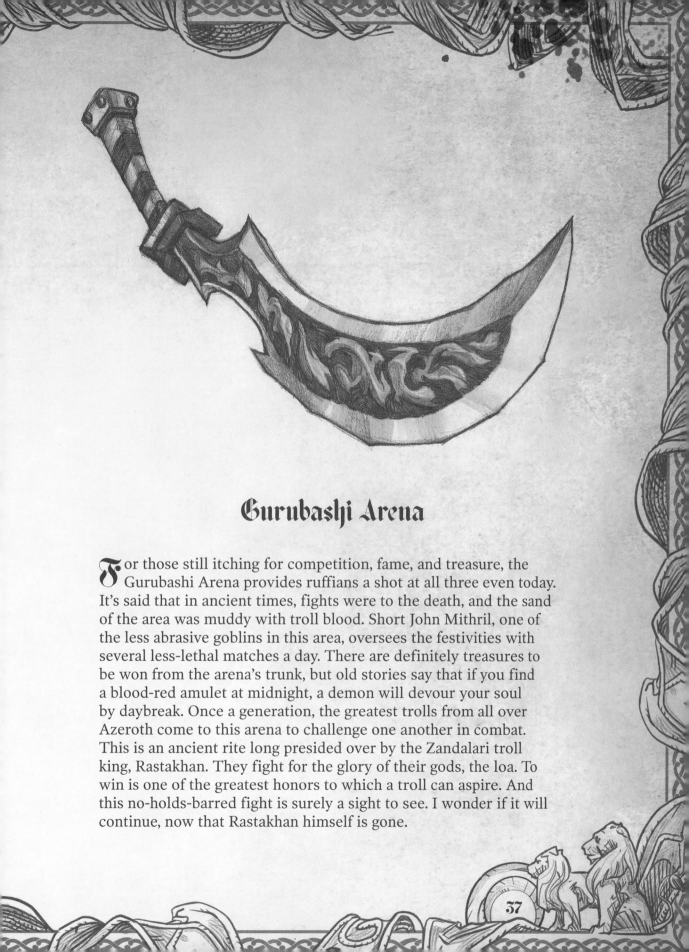

Gurubashi Arena

For those still itching for competition, fame, and treasure, the Gurubashi Arena provides ruffians a shot at all three even today. It's said that in ancient times, fights were to the death, and the sand of the area was muddy with troll blood. Short John Mithril, one of the less abrasive goblins in this area, oversees the festivities with several less-lethal matches a day. There are definitely treasures to be won from the arena's trunk, but old stories say that if you find a blood-red amulet at midnight, a demon will devour your soul by daybreak. Once a generation, the greatest trolls from all over Azeroth come to this arena to challenge one another in combat. This is an ancient rite long presided over by the Zandalari troll king, Rastakhan. They fight for the glory of their gods, the loa. To win is one of the greatest honors to which a troll can aspire. And this no-holds-barred fight is surely a sight to see. I wonder if it will continue, now that Rastakhan himself is gone.

Booty Bay

Life is cheaper here than in most places; no one is to be trusted, and the place is run by goblins. In other words, a fertile environment for information and informants, and a rogue's paradise—

RULES TO SURVIVE BOOTY BAY

I HAVE DECIDED TO PROVE MY WORTH BY ASSISTING THE SPYMASTER AND HIS RIGHT ROYAL MAJESTY KING ANDUIN BY WRITING UP THIS INFORMATIVE AND EXHAUSTIVELY RESEARCHED GUIDE TO BOOTY BAY.

Not really, no.

YOUR MAJESTY, I THINK YOU'LL LOVE IT HERE. FIRST OF ALL, YOU'VE GOT TO BE IN THE RIGHT FRAME OF MIND, AND THAT MEANS DRINKS. THE RUM HERE IS FANTASTIC, MUCH BETTER THAN THE SWILL I'M USED TO. THEY PUT LOTS OF SPICES AND FRUIT NECTAR IN IT, QUITE LOVELY. I HAD FOUR. TOOK A FIFTH WITH ME TO AMBLE ABOUT. ALL ON MY OWN, I FERRETED OUT SOME OF SHAW'S CONTACTS. I THOUGHT NARKK WAS ONE, BUT IT TURNS OUT HE ONLY SELLS PARROTS. MINE IS NAMED MATHIAS. I RAN ACROSS ANOTHER GOBLIN, THIS ONE A FRIENDLY BLOKE WITH THE FLASHY NAME OF LANDRO LONGSHOT. TURNS OUT HE'S THE MANAGER OF THE BLACK FLAME, A DELIGHTFULLY MYSTERIOUS ORGANIZATION SPECIALIZING IN "HARD-TO-FIND ITEMS, GLADIATORIAL COMBAT, AND LUCRATIVE GAMES OF CHANCE." I PROMISED I'D LOOK HIM UP. I ALWAYS WIN, IF YOU KNOW WHAT I MEAN. A BIT ODD, THOUGH. HE ASKED ME ABOUT SOMEONE NAMED PRINCESS POOBAH. I DECIDED THAT I'D BEST BE POLITE ABOUT A PRINCESS, LIKING MY HEAD ON MY SHOULDERS AS I DO, SO I SAID SHE WAS QUITE A CHARMING PERSON. AND DO YOU KNOW WHAT HE SAID? "AH YES, KING MUKLA WAS SMITTEN BY HER. SUCH A DELICATE, BEAUTIFUL TAUREN." AND THEN HE STARTED TELLING ME ALL THESE INTERESTING THINGS, JUST LIKE THAT. NO IDEA WHY.

The king doesn't need to know this

My least favorite informant in all of Azeroth.

Why are you like this?

An informant passphrase, you beautiful but ridiculous dolt.

XOXO, CAPTAIN FLYNN FAIRWIND

Janeiro's Point

Ships coming into the Booty Bay harbor used to be greeted by an open-armed statue of an unknown goblin. Regrettably, the Cataclysm damaged only part of this structure. With the revelation that the statue was hollow, we've discovered all kinds of things in its innards: captives, animals, squatters, illicit substances, rotted bodies, eloping couples, and, once, a tarnished crown. It's a mess, I fear, but one we must regularly investigate.

GIVE IT A GOOD POLISH AND I'LL WAGER I'D LOOK SMASHING.
"KING FLYNN THE FIRST." WONDER WHOSE IT WAS?
MAYBE THAT LOVELY PRINCESS POOBAH'S.

IV
Burning Steppes

This foreboding territory has long been the home of many of our greatest enemies: the orcs, the Dark Iron dwarves, and one particularly dangerous black dragon. Over two centuries ago, the Dark Iron dwarf clan settled here after they were exiled from Ironforge, carving out a new city for themselves. The eternal power their Sorcerer-Thane Thaurissan so desired came at a steep price: liberating the chaotic elemental Firelord Ragnaros. The Firelord's reentry into our world was violent, destroying much of the Redridge Mountains and creating a volcano formed of, well, black rock. To say "thank you" to the Dark Irons for freeing him from the Firelands, Ragnaros enslaved them.

Blackrock Mountain

There are numerous inhabited areas deep within these black stones; the place feels endless and labyrinthine. Many—too many—agents haven't returned.

Inside this unnaturally created volcano is some of the greatest work ever wrought by the dwarves. Stairs and passageways, sculptures, giant chains, and massive caverns—all would be magnificent to behold if the site were not so deadly. After the Second War, a new threat took hold here: the Blackrock orcs, who had come through the Dark Portal. Brutal and arrogant, their leader Blackhand must have thought the name "Blackrock" had been given to the mountain in anticipation of their arrival. A bargain was struck between the Dark Irons and the Blackrocks; the dwarves descended even deeper into the mountain, while the orcs occupied the higher levels. Like many bargains, it was never intended to be kept.

Blackwing Lair

One cannot discuss Blackrock Mountain without mentioning the black dragons, who have earned a section all to themselves: Blackwing Lair. One in particular dispensed an appalling amount of destruction from this place—Nefarian, son of Deathwing and brother to the aforementioned Onyxia. They were a busy pair of siblings, both deceptive and cunning. While Onyxia was stirring up trouble in Stormwind, Nefarian was obsessed with following in his father's gigantic footsteps by achieving what his father could not— the combination of the essences of all dragons. Thus he created a monstrous hybrid flight in Blackwing Lair: the chromatic dragons.

This twisted dragonflight wasn't the only malevolent experiment performed here without regard for the subjects. Nefarian's labs were infamous, and with good cause. He corrupted and enslaved the valiant red dragon Vaelastrasz, forcing him to attack those who had been friends. One of his creations, the two-headed Chromaggus, survived to become a dutiful protector of the lair. Even the bones of slain dragons were cobbled together to do Nefarian's bidding. With such cruelty about, something as seemingly helpless as a dragon's egg could be deadly.

Nefarian's enemy was Ragnaros, and his "allies" were the orcs. He operated from the upper part of the mountain's spire, with his lair heavily protected. When he was killed in his sanctuary, the threat did not end. He was brought back as an undead abomination and settled in at Blackwing Descent where he continued his experiments— including raising Onyxia from the dead. Eventually, thankfully, he was killed yet again. Reminders of him, his plans, and his followers turn up in the oddest places sometimes. Rumor has it his head is still lying about, and it makes sense. Who would want to go to the trouble to move something so heavy and awkward in this dangerous environment? Certainly not an SI:7 agent. For the safety of our world and our people, harsh as it is to say, I will not apologize for being pleased the black dragonflight is nearly extinct.*

TOO RIGHT, MATE.

Person of Interest: Wrathion

I know of at least three black dragons who remain. One is Sabellian, who is on Outland and poses no current danger. The two on Azeroth are Ebonhorn, who takes the form of a Highmountain tauren, and a much more active—and dangerous—one named Wrathion. Both claim they are uncorrupted black dragons. However, Wrathion's "purity" was the result of an experiment. I'm not ready to say yet if it worked, that he is truly uncorrupted. He insists to want only what is best for Azeroth. His early behavior—getting a teenaged Anduin to trust him—ended up with his betrayal and assault of the prince, the liberation of Garrosh Hellscream, AND throwing us to the Iron Horde. He has recently returned and has in fact done a great service to our world by helping rid it of the Old God N'Zoth. While I'm grateful, SI:7 is still watching him and his Blacktalon agents very closely.

* *Spymaster's Update: It has reached my ears that recently another attempt was made to raise the evil black dragon siblings. It was thwarted by valiant heroes, thankfully. In a thorough investigation of the lair, our agents found references to similar experiments that may predate Nefarian. But the evidence is incomplete and subject to errors in translation. We have collected the material for further study.*

AND PRAY EXPLAIN WHAT'S WRONG WITH LIKING WINE AND GEMS AND . . . OH. I SEE.

Blackrock Depths

The depths of this mountain have housed a veritable prison full of miscreants and monsters—both literal and figurative. High Interrogator Gerstahn, for instance, was a noblewoman who loved her luxuries: clothing, wine, gems, and the finest torture tools for her work. I can't say I see the appeal in ruby-encrusted pliers.

Shadowforge City, the capital of the Dark Iron dwarves, is located here as well. Its vastness rivals that of Ironforge itself. Emperor Dagran Thaurissan, a direct descendant of that rash Sorcerer-Thane, captured Magni Bronzebeard's daughter Moira,✳ intending to use her as a hostage. Instead, they fell in love. When he was killed here, Queen Moira was devastated and furious. She does not wish the Alliance well, and the Dark Irons remain our enemies.✳✳

Many invaluable imperial artifacts have been retrieved from Blackrock Depths over the years. Most noteworthy is the truly legendary **Ironfoe**.✳✳✳ Its crafter, Master Franclorn Forgewright— who built the Stonewrought Dam and much of Blackrock Depths itself—gave it to an ancestor of the late, much missed Marshal Windsor. The Dark Irons took it from Windsor when they captured and imprisoned him. In its day, it felled countless orcs. Perhaps Dagran should have made better use of his **Guiding Stave of Wisdom** and avoided a thorough beatdown.

I'm told that the Grim Guzzler tavern and its Brewfest, here at what feels like the bottom of the world, make the journeying worthwhile. I wouldn't know, as I largely abstain from anything that clouds the mind.

OH COME ON. ALE IS THE ELIXIR OF THE ARTISTS! JUST LOOK AT THIS MASTERPIECE I MADE OF YOU!

* *Spymaster's Update #1:* Queen-Regent Moira Thaurissan has returned and now represents the Dark Iron clan in absentia as a member of the Council of Three Hammers.

** *Spymaster's Update #2:* Dark Iron dwarves are now official members of the Alliance. With contentions and disagreements subsiding, we may have found ourselves with new stalwart allies.

*** *Spymaster's Update #3:* Ironfoe was taken but has been reclaimed. Now Thaelin Darkanvil is its keeper.

WITH HOW QUICKLY ALLEGIANCES CHANGE HERE ON THE MAINLAND, YOU'VE NO RIGHT SAYING PIRATES ARE THE SHIFTY ONES.

Molten Core

There is a nightmarish place beneath the aforementioned bottom of the world: the sulfuric Molten Core, the gateway from the Firelands to our world. Ragnaros himself held his seat of power here. Those who were courageous—or foolhardy—enough to challenge him had to overcome vicious flamewakers, among the most dangerous elementals in the Firelands; corehounds and their monstrous father, Magmadar, creatures of both fire and earth; and even Ragnaros's Majordomo Executus, second only to the Firelord himself. Only a small army of well-prepared champions even had the slightest chance.

His weapon was a terrible one: a mighty hammer named **Sulfuras**. It was called "the Hand of Ragnaros," as he never released it until his defeat here in the Core. Miraculously, when Ragnaros was reborn in his own realm of the Firelands, brave adventurers and soldiers of both the Horde and Alliance defeated him once again. His weapon now reflects the same loss as **Sulfuras, the Extinguished Hand**. In this perhaps lies our best proof that he is, finally, dead.

In such a dark place as Blackrock Mountain, a little bit of lightness is a welcome reprieve. Finkle Einhorn provided it. The fellow has had more close scrapes—and has survived them all, thus far—than any one gnome I know. He's tested a lava suit, been devoured by a corehound called "The Beast," was later freed by some adventurers, barely escaped the Beast's mate (and pups), and apparently had time to create (and lose) a mace and an extremely well-made knife. He may be the most eclectic informant we have.

*WHY ARE THEY ALWAYS "BADLANDS"?
WHY AREN'T THERE ANY "GOODLANDS," OR
"PLEASANT PLACES," OR SOME SUCH? MISSED
TOURIST OPPORTUNITY, IF YOU ASK ME.*

~~~~ V ~~~~

Badlands

A place whose name suits it perfectly. The Badlands are located in Khaz Modan, between Stormwind and Dun Morogh and easily mistaken as Alliance territory. To be sure, there are a lot of dwarves here. They are, by and large, either prospectors or members of the Explorers' League. I find it interesting how adaptable dwarves are. They thrive in the cold mountains but seem just as vigorous and active in the jungles of Stranglethorn or here in the desert.

There used to be a Horde outpost here called Kargath that was destroyed in the Cataclysm. The Horde has since rebuilt it, naming it New Kargath. To the east are two towns occupied by the goblin Steamwheedle Cartel—Fuselight and the failed-attempt port of Fuselight-by-the-Sea. Survival here mandates an excellent map of the ruins and the general layout, as sandstorms can sweep in and make navigation difficult. This is an extreme environment, so travel at night, sleep during the day, protect your face from the sand and winds, and bring plenty of water. Or a mage.

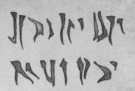

Uldaman

Uldaman is essentially a massive vault created by the titan keepers. It is an excellent place to pause (with care and safety) and reflect on our small place in the grand scheme of things. Humbling, to be sure. There are significant artifacts here for those willing to look for them—mainly archaeologists and fortune hunters, who are slowly digging up this ruin of a titan-forged city. And of course, we're interested in what *they're* interested in. As I said, you'll find several of the Explorers' League here, but their Horde equivalent, the Reliquary, is also more than eager to locate and procure ancient treasures.

Rumor has it that there's a secret room to be discovered here—the Chamber of Khaz'mul. Conveniently for the sake of a good story, it's impossible to enter without a special artifact—the **Staff of Prehistoria**. Not only that, but the staff was broken into two pieces that must be found—the **Shaft of Tsol** and the **Gni'kiv Medallion**. Place the completed staff in a certain part of the map chamber, and it will activate a magical door. If the stories hold true, daring adventurers must fight off Ironaya, a titan keeper standing ready behind the door. There are artifacts aplenty to be found in Uldaman . . . but I've yet to see anyone carrying the Staff of Prehistoria.

The most valuable things to have been unearthed in this dangerous place are the **Discs of Norgannon**, located in the deepest chamber of Uldaman called Khaz'goroth's Seat. They are not portable, but we have obtained accurate, if much smaller, copies of them. They contain a wealth of hitherto unknown information about the titan's experiments with the earthen, the ancestors of our dwarven friends, some of it startling and strange. Titanic keepers created the earthen to assist with the tasks of shaping the deep places of the earth. It seems that they were formed by a "subterranean being matrix," which I imagine is a sort of template. The Discs speak of a corruption, the "curse of flesh," which resulted in the dwarves evolving into the form we know now. Brann Bronzebeard is the dwarf whose brain you should pick if you want to know more. We've only scratched the surface of what the Discs have to tell us, and all interested parties should ensure that sensitive information doesn't fall into the wrong hands. As for the details . . . I prefer to think of the dwarves more as a people than a matrix, and staunch friends at that.

Armor Aside: *THE EARTHFURY*

While a shaman's duty is to the protection of the earth, they can still invoke the elements' wrath. The cracked rock and molten lava of the Earthfury armor is the most physical example of a shaman's power I can think of. While wearing these powerful robes, the shaman's totems reach incredible distances. Every rock, tree, and blade of grass seems to respect its power.

HA!

AND THEY SAY THE TITANS HAVE NO SENSE OF HUMOR.

The titan keeper tasked with guarding the Discs was named Archaedas—a being of few words, which I respect. He slept until someone awakened him by activating the keystone and attempting to break into the vault. He fought quite fiercely, but eventually was destroyed by ambitious adventurers.✱ His weapons were left behind, perhaps out of fear or respect—they include the **Rockpounder**, a massive mace that requires both hands to wield and renders the bearer more likely to strike true; **Stoneslayer**, a sword that strikes as hard as you'd expect for a titan build; and finally, a ring that someone simply dubbed the **Archaedic Stone**. Many powerful enchantments are woven into this stone; it is an unpredictable thing. I'm told that one never knows which enchantment will manifest at any given time. Sometimes it offers the wielder great strength, or resistance to fire, for example. I pity adventures hoping for an enchantment that makes them agile enough for a quick exit and instead finding themselves intelligent enough to realize they're doomed.

A LITTLE BIT OF SMUGNESS. EH?
I LIKE IT.

✱ *Spymaster's Update: Rumors have reached me that Archaedas might not have been destroyed, merely disabled. I suppose the old saying is true—you can't keep a good titan servant down.*

VI

Ironforge

Ironforge is one of the most ancient cities of Azeroth, home to both an active population and a rich culture. The dwarves who carved it, bit by bit, from the mountain continue to be stalwart and reliable. Stormwind is fortunate to call them allies and friends. There's a lot going on here all hours of the day and night: the Great Forge never shuts down, and the Hall of Explorers waits to entertain, educate, and, especially with SI:7 agents, inform. I would tread lightly in the place called the Forlorn Cavern, however. Dark things do go on there. You'll see rogues and warlocks about, but no notification of any import has reached my ears from this corner. Something to keep a close eye on.

The Great Forge

Few settings are as bold and clearly identifiable with their race as the Great Forge of Ironforge is with dwarves. In fact, I'm told the name of the city was chosen to honor it. The scale is gigantic, especially when you consider that dwarves are . . . not. The Great Anvil, directly in the center of the Forge area, has been used for centuries unknown. Many weapons and objects of beauty have been crafted upon it, including the **Ashbringer**, which Magni Bronzebeard himself fashioned. It's loud, and hot, and cheerful, and is not merely the center of Ironforge, it's the central part of life here. Most citizens pass by the Forge regularly, and the keeper of the Forge, Myolor Sunderfury, along with the many trainers, sees and hears quite a bit. Visitors come by to behold the spectacle, rendering this place a fine spot for eavesdropping in plain sight to hear news from all over the Alliance.

SO ARE PUBS AND BARS, MATE.
I THINK YOU SERIOUSLY UNDERUSE THIS OPTION.

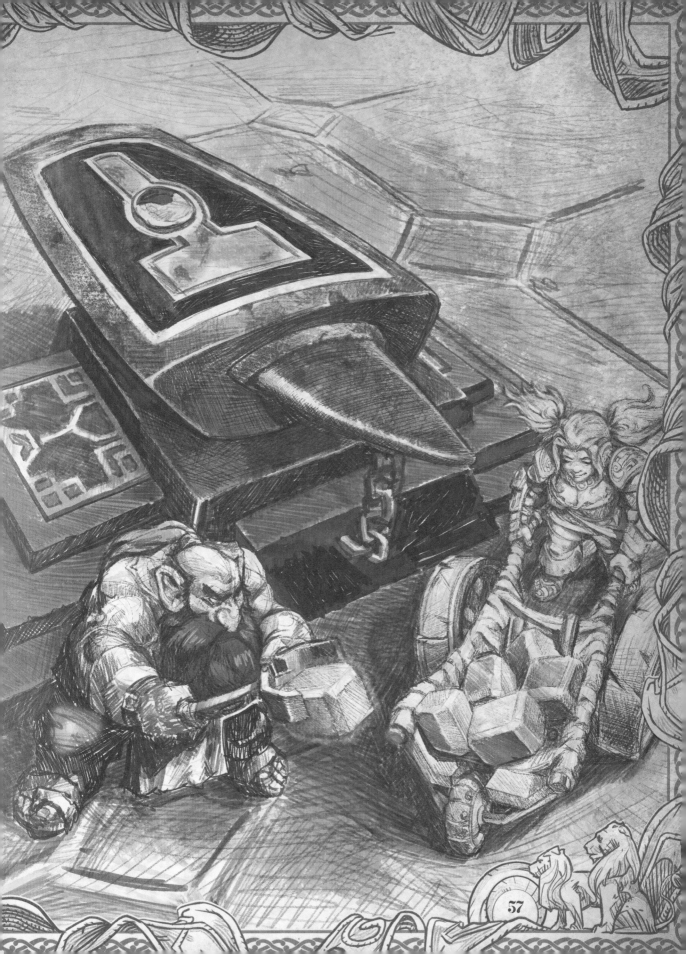

"SAVAGE PASSIONS," EY?

The Hall of Explorers and the Library

At first glance, the Hall of Explorers appears to be nothing more than a museum of interesting artifacts that the League has collected. The skeleton of a pteradon is ominously suspended from the ceiling. Another massive skeleton—this one a replica—demonstrates just how gigantic the fabled ram Toothgnasher really was. The stuff of folklore and tall tales, this enormous creature holds a warm place in dwarven hearts. Children are told that if they are good, the spirit of Toothgnasher will give them a ride on his back; if they are bad, he will toss them on his horns. This may account for how well behaved dwarven children generally are. One disturbing display is the enormous skull of the dragon Tyrannistrasz, who may have been the elder consort of Alexstrasza. I understand there are many archeologists in the Explorers League who support the idea of returning the skull to the red dragonflight.

As stated earlier, using the Forlorn Cavern for SI:7 purposes would be too obvious, so in Ironforge, we have a twist. Few know the extent of the excellent (and unofficial) relationship between SI:7 and the Explorers' League. Both organizations traverse Azeroth, uncovering, keeping, and occasionally sharing information. High Explorer Muninn Magellas often has news for us and leaves valuable missives in a slot beneath the rug upon entry. It sounds contrived, but Magellas's method and information have yet to fail me. There is a certain shelf of books, all in the back, that are encoded. We also come here from time to time to speak with librarian Mae Paledust. The place is filled with rare tomes, and she knows where to find what you need.

Bill Spearshaker is the keeper of the code books. In order to get the title of the coded one you're looking for, you must quote a title from one of those potboilers he claims to have authored. I think he does it to sell more books and enjoys seeing my discomfort at uttering words like "I'm In Love with a Robot" or "Savage Passions." Nonetheless, and somewhat inexplicably, this bizarre choice of code has been successful.

The High Seat

Many significant places are arranged in a ring around the Great Forge, like a wheel with the Forge as its center hub. Directly across from the Hall of Explorers is the High Seat, where Magni Bronzebeard once ruled. It's large enough to hold several people and can get full when petitioners are being heard. It is still odd to me to see three dwarves here rather than Magni. But the Council of Three Hammers seems to be working together very well. Moira Thaurissan, as Magni Bronzebeard's undisputed heir, came to Ironforge with anger and a desire to have the dwarven race under her thumb, but eventually agreed to the concept of each dwarf clan having its own representative. It is presumed that when her son, Dagran Thaurissan II, comes of age, he will rule not only Ironforge, but Shadowforge City as well, uniting the dwarves in a way no single ruler ever has. Of course, that future remains to be seen.✳

Alongside Moira, Muradin represents the Bronzebeard clan that has ruled Ironforge for so very long. Falstad Wildhammer was persuaded to leave the Hinterlands and speak for his people here. My sources tell me that treats brought for his gryphons, Swiftwing, Keenclaw, and Sharpbeak, will warm his heart and earn his trust. Certainly worth a few wolf steaks or a rabbit or three.

✳ *Spymaster's Update: Moira has settled into her role well over the years, and, considering how useful the Dark Irons have been to the Alliance, in retrospect it seems odd that we did not agree to her request earlier.*

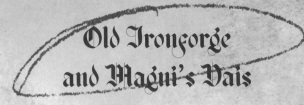

Old Ironforge and Magni's Dais

The door to Old Ironforge, known now as the Assembly of Thanes, is deep below the High Seat and has been firmly closed for years. In Magni's effort to aid the troubled elementals that foreshadowed the Cataclysm and the return of Deathwing, the dwarven king opened up a part of the old city to enact a rite to speak to the elements by "making him one with the earth." Everyone assumed that was only a figure of speech. Tragically, it was not. To this day, the noble Magni Bronzebeard, transformed to diamond, stands rooted on what has become known as "Magni's Dais."✶

✶ *Spymaster's Update: I am pleased to update this report by saying that Magni has broken free of his crystalline chamber . . . after a fashion. He lives, but he is still "one with the earth" in that he remains diamond, not flesh. Glittering shards from his liberation litter the floor and stairs. A scheming thief might believe they could steal piece or two, but the area is full of armored guards. I would strongly advise against this, tempting though it may be, not only for the safety of one's hand, but also for our continued good relationship with the dwarven people.*

NOW WHO WOULD POCKET SOMETHING LIKE THAT? CERTAINLY NOT THE LIKES OF ME. NO SIREE!

Gnomeregan

Once, the gnomes were forced to abandon their home of Gnomeregan. The creatures known as troggs—ugly, vicious precursors of the original earthen—had infested it. These creatures were sleeping harmlessly within the earth until they were awakened when titan sites like Uldaman were disturbed. Much more physically powerful than our weaker but brilliant friends, the troggs drove the gnomes out of Gnomeregan. In a last, desperate attempt, High Tinker Gelbin Mekkatorque listened to his old friend, Mekgineer Thermaplugg, and reluctantly decided to flood the infested areas of Gnomeregan with lethal radiation. But Thermaplugg was a traitor—soon, the troggs were more violent than ever, while eighty percent of gnomes perished. More were mutated into leper gnomes. The leper gnomes still dwell inside much of Gnomeregan, but the remaining gnomes were welcomed into Ironforge by the dwarves. They formed a section of the city called Tinkertown, where many of them still reside. In recent years, they have managed to reclaim the surface of Gnomeregan and part of its interior, which they have dubbed New Tinkertown. I for one am glad "old" Tinkertown is still lively and filled with gnomish energy. It is my favorite place for supplementing the ranks of SI:7. The gnomes' intelligence, curious natures, nimble fingers, and small stature make them perfect spies. There is a tremendous benefit to appearing cute and harmless.

ALWAYS WORKS FOR ME.

Reclaiming even part of Gnomeregan was no small task—many courageous people were willing to risk their lives to aid the gnomes. The radiation posed a constant danger, as did those affected by it. The leper gnomes were driven mad and were easily recruited by the jealous Thermaplugg, who himself had been twisted into a leper gnome and rendered insane. The troggs were fiercer than ever. And at least one water elemental who had made its way inside became a seething creature of viscous fallout. Thermaplugg threw everything he had against the would-be liberators: twisted machines, such as the **Electrocutioner**, a tank with mechanical spider legs driven by a maddened follower. Some precious armaments, however, were recovered as well: a leg from the Electrocutioner can, helpfully, double as an extremely effective sword. Near where a contaminated water elemental resided, one could find the lifesaving staff **Hydrocane**, which enables its bearer to breathe underwater. And Thermaplugg, as wretched and murderous as he was in life, carried some unique equipment with him, such as the **Electromagnetic Gigaflux Reactivator**, a helmet that appears to harness the very power of lightning for a time. These artifacts have been returned to Tinkertown for safekeeping. It is extremely satisfying to know that the good gnomish people have finally started to come home.

To Spymaster Shaw and his companion Captain Flynn Fairwind,

Moira Thaurissan, Queen-Regent of the Dark Iron clan, Muradin Bronzebeard, Representative of the Bronzebeard clan, and Falstad Wildhammer, High Thane of the Wildhammer clan, do extend the warmest of welcomes to our glorious city. In the interests of continuing to strengthen the bonds between Ironforge and Stormwind, we do hereby once again open our vaults, so that the Spymaster may reassure himself that our collection of artifacts, weaponry, and documents is being well cared for and properly protected. We invite both good gentlemen to enjoy our hospitality during their visit, partake of our fine brew, and relax in the company of our kind citizens. As always, we remain ready to assist our good friends from Stormwind whenever they call upon us.

—THE THREE HAMMERS

VII
Arathi Highlands

So many have died here that it's a surprise the place isn't crawling with ghosts. At least the most recent bloody battle ended with an Alliance victory, thanks to High Exarch Turalyon, Muradin Bronzebeard, and Danath Trollbane's leadership—as well as the steadfastness of every soldier who stood on this ground.

The Arathi Highlands could be called humanity's birthplace. This area was an empire, and the city of Strom was once the center of it. For a time, it became the center of the world, at least for the Alliance. Since then, much has fallen into disrepair. The old seat of power, Stromgarde, once the home of Danath's uncle Thoras Trollbane, was practically in ruins. We had to rebuild it, stone by stone, timber by timber. Then we created engines of war, barracks for soldiers, all the while fighting back the Horde, who was vying for the tactical location. The forest troll, Nimar the Slayer, took many with him when he died, as did the wretched kobold, Overseer Krix. (Though the little donkey that was intended to be Krix's dinner soon found a good home.) From their monstrous war machine Doom's Howl, to full-on sieges of our castle, the Horde made our victory a dear one. Now the question remains: What to do with what we have created in a world where an armistice might actually lead to true peace? The soldiers are home, but there are guards here still. Just in case.

Arathi Basin

The nearby Arathi Basin, rich in vital resources, has long been a site of contention between the Horde and the Alliance. Many of our soldiers have come home with evidence of their courage in the form of the **Talisman of Arathor**. Others remember fighting with the purple glow of the **Ironbark Staff** all around them or tell stories of how the powerful **Sageclaw**—a dagger of both cold steel and magic—saved their lives. Many veterans of these battles got to know the supply officer, Samuel Hawke, quite well, as he was the one who rewarded their martial skills with armor, weapons, and magical items of one sort or another, so that they would be even safer on the battlefield.

Armor Aside:
FELHEART RAIMENT

The eerie horns of the Felheart Raiment will always be unsettling to me. I've had my fair share of exchanges with demons and the like—why anyone would willingly cooperate with the monsters is beyond me. Still, I must admit, the display of resilience and vigor by warlocks donning this accursed armor is . . . truly frightening.

Stromgarde Keep

Stromgarde Keep was a seat of power for hundreds of years before the death of King Thoras. It became a crucial defensive hold for the Alliance during the Fourth War. While we protected and rebuilt it as our stronghold, the Horde was quick to take Northold Manor for theirs. The abandoned farm, once a hotbed of Syndicate activity, was quickly turned into a powerful Horde base of operations in Arathi. Proudly, the Alliance triumphed here in the end. I've heard that some members of the Horde believe those who fell in battle in these highlands here now haunt the ruins of Ar'gorok, angry at their defeat and craving revenge.

The Trollbanes have had . . . interesting relationships with death. And undeath. Their family crypt has been far busier than most. Danath's uncle, the aforementioned King Thoras Trollbane, was murdered by his son Galen. He died some time after his dear friend, King Terenas Menethil II, perished in the same horrible manner. Galen was killed by the Horde, only to be raised as a Forsaken to serve Sylvanas. Unable to stay loyal to anyone, it seems, Galen led a rebellion to reclaim Stromgarde. He failed in this effort and was targeted by the Ebon Blade, who killed him and then proceeded to raise his father as one of their Four Horsemen.

I once overheard Danath muttering that when he died, he'd better be cremated. I don't blame him. Ashes cannot wield a weapon as the undead can.

Stromgarde Keep's church is known as the Sanctum. Danath has generously given his blessing to me to routinely survey what remains in the Sanctum's crypt. The crypt itself is easy to miss, as it's tucked away behind the church proper. For a long time, the only company King Thoras had was the mighty sword **Trol'kalar**, or "Troll Slayer." It was a precious family heirloom and a weapon of great power. Both king and sword were thought safe here, but Trol'kalar was stolen. Presently, its whereabouts are unknown.

LOVELY. NEEDED TO HAVE SOME HORDE GHOSTS! THE ALLIANCE ONES WERE GETTING DULL.

HONESTLY ALL THIS—DEATH, UNDEATH, GHOSTS, TOMBS—IS THE STUFF OF MY NIGHTMARES. THAT, AND THE ONE WHERE... I NEVER MIND.

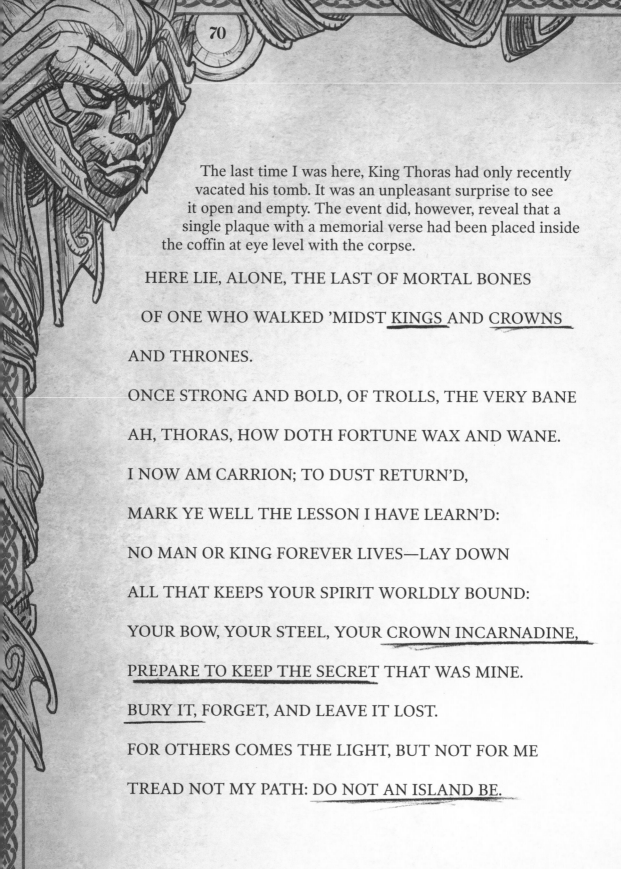

The last time I was here, King Thoras had only recently vacated his tomb. It was an unpleasant surprise to see it open and empty. The event did, however, reveal that a single plaque with a memorial verse had been placed inside the coffin at eye level with the corpse.

HERE LIE, ALONE, THE LAST OF MORTAL BONES

OF ONE WHO WALKED 'MIDST KINGS AND CROWNS

AND THRONES.

ONCE STRONG AND BOLD, OF TROLLS, THE VERY BANE

AH, THORAS, HOW DOTH FORTUNE WAX AND WANE.

I NOW AM CARRION; TO DUST RETURN'D,

MARK YE WELL THE LESSON I HAVE LEARN'D:

NO MAN OR KING FOREVER LIVES—LAY DOWN

ALL THAT KEEPS YOUR SPIRIT WORLDLY BOUND:

YOUR BOW, YOUR STEEL, YOUR CROWN INCARNADINE,

PREPARE TO KEEP THE SECRET THAT WAS MINE.

BURY IT, FORGET, AND LEAVE IT LOST.

FOR OTHERS COMES THE LIGHT, BUT NOT FOR ME

TREAD NOT MY PATH: DO NOT AN ISLAND BE.

Ravenholdt Manor

Years ago, a group called the Syndicate wandered this part of the Highlands, comprised of noblemen and their vassals who resorted to the tactics of those who should be well beneath them. It is not the first time nobility have behaved like scoundrels. I am pleased to say the Ravenholdt assassin organization led by Jorach Ravenholdt accepted SI:7's aid in routing out the Syndicate affliction, housing the base of operations out of his manor. As of this writing, Ravenholdt is currently the leader of the Uncrowned.

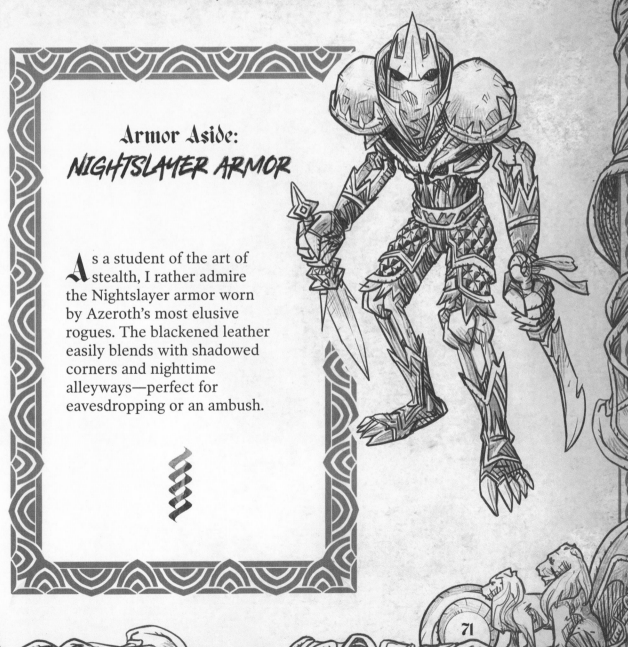

Armor Aside: NIGHTSLAYER ARMOR

As a student of the art of stealth, I rather admire the Nightslayer armor worn by Azeroth's most elusive rogues. The blackened leather easily blends with shadowed corners and nighttime alleyways—perfect for eavesdropping or an ambush.

The Gathering Graves

Compared to the battles that have been fought on this land, the tiny cemetery just south of Newstead could easily seem insignificant. But it isn't. Shortly before the Fourth War, Sylvanas agreed to King Anduin's suggestion of a gathering of Forsaken and their living kin. When Calia Menethil yielded to compassion during the event, helping those Forsaken who wished to defect, Sylvanas deemed it a betrayal. She retaliated by slaughtering the priestess and all Forsaken still on the field, leaving them to rot. It was our king who buried them and placed markers on these twelve graves. I still don't know how it all makes me feel. But every time I come to this area I pause here.

Hope is an erratic thing, a lesson I have learned well and strive to instill in all my agents. Trust in it at your peril.

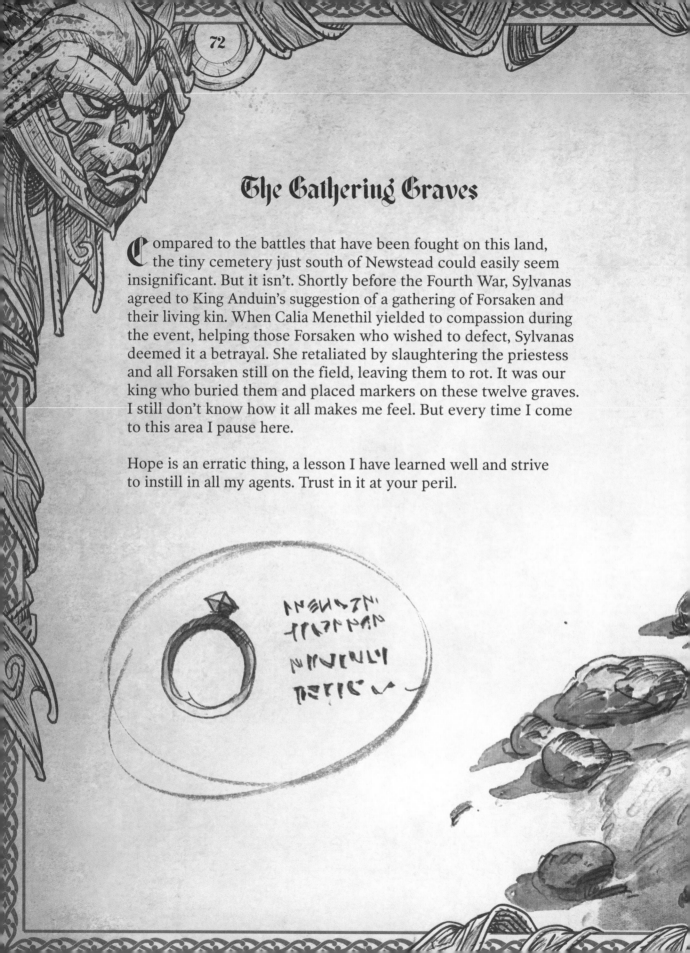

VIII
The Plaguelands
WESTERN PLAGUELANDS
Hearthglen

I find it jarring to travel from other locales in this area to this town; it's so peaceful. But Hearthglen was not spared from the attacking undead after plague-ridden grain from Andorhal was distributed. Two paladins and Lordaeron's troops arrived to turn the tide and drive the Scourge from this tranquil hamlet. Those paladins were Sir Uther the Lightbringer and his student, Prince Arthas Menethil. I wonder if the irony of that ever chafed at Arthas, all those years on the Frozen Throne.

Lord Tirion Fordring, another paladin of the Silver Hand, once had the high position of governor of the hamlet. His home was Mardenholde Keep, where a rare and precious book called *The Light and How to Swing It* was kept for a time. The tome was penned by Sir Uther himself. It was never intended for anyone other than the person it was written for: Arthas. But over time, many have benefitted from Uther's wisdom and experience. It is a tragedy that Arthas himself did not. The book was recovered from the Athenaeum in Dire Maul, and until recently was in the hands of Lorekeeper Mykos. She has graciously donated it to the paladin archives at Light's Hope Sanctum and removed the mark of the Athenaeum, allowing all paladins to read the tome.

On the wall hangs a emotional piece of art—a portrait of Tirion; his wife, Karandra; and their son, Taelan, entitled "Of Love and Family." I hear the ghost of the artist, Renfray, wanders Caer Darrow, hoping still that perhaps her old friend Tirion will come to save those long dead.* This plague was not the one Kel'Thuzad unleashed on us but rather a Scholomance experiment: a devastating illness powerful enough to wipe out the entire population and force the victims to linger on as ghosts. It appears as if this variation of the plague has run its course . . . but nonetheless, I seldom send my agents here.

ALL RIGHT. THAT'S JUST BLOODY SAD.

★ *Spymaster's Update: I regret to write that since my last entry, Tirion Fordring has joined his artist friend—and both his wife and son—in death. He died having lived a long life of honor and service; it took a monster of the Burning Legion to end him. He is interred in the Sanctum of Light, where his plaque reads:*

FRIEND, BROTHER, MENTOR. HIGHLORD FORDRING WAS A PARAGON OF THE LIGHT— AND EXEMPLAR OF WHAT ALL PALADINS STRIVE TO BE. MAY HIS SPIRIT GUIDE US IN THE DARK DAYS TO COME.

I hope it does, for those that need him. Mardenholde Keep is now a training ground, and Lieutenant Myner holds the keys to the treasures stored here. Recovered from Stratholme and on display at Mardenholde is the **Barovian family sword** and a sort of ritual hood, which I am content to observe from behind glass.

I DON'T LIKE THIS STORY, SHAW. I REALLY DON'T. WHEN WE FINISH UP AND HEAD TO A PUB, YOU OWE ME ANOTHER, LESS PAINFUL STORY. AND A PINT. MAKE IT TWO: ONE TO POUR OUT FOR THIS POOR BLOKE.

The Light and How to Swing It

Being a true paladin of the Light is both a blessing and a burden. A blessing, in that the Light will come when you ask it to, and you may save the lives of injured comrades while fighting your enemies. A burden, in that you must be willing to shoulder more than you think you can, to do all that the Light tasks you, be it small or great. I know your passion, Arthas, your earnestness and enthusiasm. These are important qualities, for paladins must strike down their foes, not just protect their allies. But these traits must be tempered, with prayer and meditation. Only a calm mind will provide clear actions; only a peaceful heart may be truly infused with the Light. I hope one day you will pause long enough to take a breath and ask for help from the Light, and that it may rush to you joyfully with the answers you seek.

Scholomance

It's unsurprising that the plague was tested here, or that some disquieting information comes from this truly evil place. I regret to report that, at the date of this entry, Scholomance is still in operation as a school of necromancy. I never shirk my duty, but I cannot say that I envy the Argent Crusade; the investigation of this place falls under their purview. One might think we would grow indifferent to the idea of undeath. One would be wrong. Scholomance also demonstrates the worst that can happen when nobles become too greedy and too fearful of losing their land, titles, and riches. For decades, House Barov owned the land of Caer Darrow, Brill, Southshore, and Tarren Mill. Not content with that, they made a deal with the infamous mage Kel'Thuzad, who was at that time the leader of the Cult of the Damned. Their manor was turned into Scholomance, and they were turned into the undead. According to the Argent Crusade reports, some of the Barovs are still there; Darkmaster Gandling has many puppets to play with. One might meet Jandice Barov—or perhaps many Jandice Barovs, as she was a master of illusion in life and appears just as strong in death. Near her dwelling, you could find one of the ritual hoods said to be worn by students or members of the Cult of the Damned. I advised it remain locked in that foul manor. A foul creature named Rattlegore—a golem comprised of an unsettling variety of bones—was thought dispatched in Andorhal. He has been risen or been rebuilt—I'm not sure of the correct term; regardless he is as dangerous and disturbing as ever.

"THE SCHOOL FOR CRUEL." HA! CRACK MYSELF UP.

But at least one person escaped: a Forsaken rogue named Lilian Voss.*
Once the daughter of High Priest Benedictus Voss of the Scarlet
Crusade, she was raised into undeath, becoming the very thing the
Crusade hates most. When she was captured by the Scarlet Crusade,
her own father disowned her and ordered her execution. She turned
the tables and executed him instead. For a long time, she seems to
have tried to find her place in the world, working with Alliance and
Horde alike to destroy the Scarlet Crusade. She entered Scholomance
at one point, only to be taken by Darkmaster Gandling. She did
escape, leaving behind some gear and a necklace that seems to glow
with a dark blaze. She is definitely someone to keep an eye on.**

* *Spymaster's Update #1: Lilian Voss is now a member in good
standing with the Uncrowned.*

** *Spymaster's Update #2: Lilian Voss presently speaks for the
Forsaken on the Horde council, since Sylvanas has abandoned
them. She has also been meeting with Calia Menethil, who has
undergone her own challenges with undeath. I have hopes of a
positive solution regarding the Lordaeron situation.*

Andorhal

This is where it began: plague in grains of wheat. Such small things, to have done so much. If only we had known; it is so easy to burn a sack or a cart. Perhaps even if we did know, a bag would have escaped detection. That could have been enough. I believe that, like Stratholme, this is an important and sobering place for my agents to see. This dark time will always weigh heavy on our hearts.

Andorhal in the Western Plaguelands was the site of the first major outbreak of the plague in the Eastern Kingdoms. A dreadful distinction if there ever was one. But the Eastern Plaguelands has certainly seen its share of both the noblest and the cruelest of humanity. While the ravages of the plague linger, they are fading, slowly; the presence of the Argent Crusade is scattered throughout. These towers and other areas are oases for those who traverse this land. While the Scarlet Crusade has retreated, the damage they did was great. They serve to warn us that going to any extreme must be undertaken with caution, or we will become what we hate.

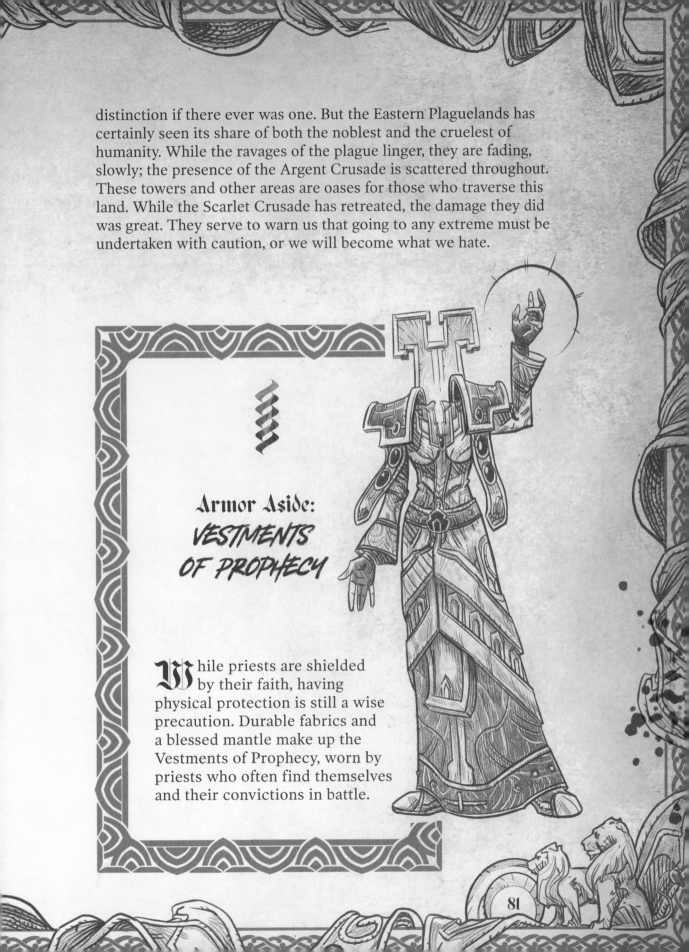

Armor Aside: VESTMENTS OF PROPHECY

While priests are shielded by their faith, having physical protection is still a wise precaution. Durable fabrics and a blessed mantle make up the Vestments of Prophecy, worn by priests who often find themselves and their convictions in battle.

EASTERN PLAGUELANDS
Marris Stead

It is hard to believe, but Nathanos Marris, who now boasts the name of Blightcaller,✱ was once on our side. He was a master strategist and, as the only human ranger lord, served at the side of Ranger-General Sylvanas Windrunner of Silvermoon. As countless did, he died by the hand of the Scourge only to be raised into undeath. When the Lich King's power waned, Sylvanas searched for him and brought him into her service. Certainly, he was her champion; whatever else they might have been to each other appears lost to undeath, along with their compassion and morality.

I endeavor to stay as detached as possible, but I confess there are times when it proves challenging. I had heard rumors of his new . . . status and sent five of my finest agents to investigate. We never learned what happened to four of them, and the fifth was murdered in his sleep shortly after making it back alive. In his sleep. *An SI:7 agent.*

We knew we were up against someone extraordinarily dangerous—and cunning. It was no surprise that it was Nathanos. No matter, we will find him and put him and his blighted hounds out of their—and our—misery.✱✱

✱ *Spymaster's Update #1: I am pleased to report that, thanks to some courageous Alliance citizens, Nathanos Marris, known after death as the Blightcaller, will trouble us no more.*

✱✱ *Spymaster's Update #2: There is little fate loves more than hubris. Sylvanas once again has her champion, and his mind, at least, was not damaged by undeath. He remains as brilliant a strategist as he ever was. His new body is stronger and in better condition than before. No matter. We will still bring him down.*

Stratholme

SI:7 agents are often faced with life-or-death decisions that must be made in a heartbeat. The right decision can mean salvation or doom. Arthas was faced with one such. The plagued grain had reached the city and had been consumed by many. There was more than one way to handle it—ways to grant salvation to some, if not all. But Arthas, enraged and untested, chose doom. He and those who followed him gutted the entire city of Stratholme, slaughtered every one of the townsfolk. It was not only a brutal decision, but a futile one, as many fell beneath his sword only to rise again. Arthas's life—and death—was the consequence of poor choices, some for the best of reasons.

For a destroyed city, Stratholme is very active. In addition to the now-undead citizens, there are a few yet living, surviving somehow. Others took up residence after its fall. Two of these were Balnazzar, a majorly devious demon . . . and Baron Rivendare, a major ~~██~~

Both adjectives could be applied to Balnazzar. At first, it was a family affair, as Balnazzar was one of three dreadlords, along with Varimathras, who "served" Sylvanas for some time until eventually betraying her, and Detheroc. I insist that this hated name be mentioned in every new agent's initial briefing as a reminder to always, always be wary. Detheroc captured and impersonated me to trick my own people into murdering Amber Kearnen, my best agent and my best friend. To have one's appearance used for such a brutal purpose . . . Let's just say it is a constant reminder that I should form no personal attachments.

? ? ?

**I'M SORRY. MATE.
I DIDN'T KNOW.**

Light's Hope Chapel

Aptly named, this chapel has been a beacon and comfort to those who journey here. Beneath the chapel is the Sanctum of Light, a place for the Knights of the Silver Hand to congregate. Many paladins of the past take their final rest here, their bodies safe from the grips of any forces who would use them for dark purposes. The walls of this place are covered with famous weapons, and its halls have made room to store many of the artifacts that have been recovered from Scholomance, Stratholme, and the Plaguelands in general.

Probably the most dangerous exhibits here were the ones recovered from Balnazzar's body—especially his weapons. They are far too dangerous to be displayed anywhere else; they need holy warding and are too tempting for people to resist them.

Demonshear was the greatsword Balnazzar himself wielded when he masqueraded as Grand Crusader Saidan Dathrohan. It is said that sometimes the blade releases dark energy that strikes hard and weakens the victim more as time passes. The **Hammer of the Grand Crusader** is likewise dangerous in the wrong hands . . . and sometimes in better ones, helping to improve its owner's speed, power, and endurance.

The **Crown of Tyranny** might be useful in battle, increasing one's reactions and accuracy, but it is rumored that those who don it will, over time, go mad from dreams of the Twisting Nether. Similar things are whispered about the **Shroud of Nathrezim**. I would not drape such a foul thing over my shoulders for all the gold in Azeroth.

The most interesting, and possibly the most dangerous, artifact is the **Book of the Dead**. It is ancient beyond imagining, and I am certain only magic is holding together something so fragile a mere touch should dissolve it into dust. The cover and spine are made from dried skin—from which animal, no one knows—and decorated with the bones of small creatures. Blood is used for ink to write the runes and incantations it contains. Scholars have theorized that the blood was drawn from living creatures at the moment they were sacrificed. We have copied the runes in more mundane ink and keep them heavily warded in the Cathedral so that we might recognize it if, Light forbid, we see this language written elsewhere.

The other recent inhabitant—or *inhabitants*, rather—of Stratholme are the Rivendares, father and son. Baron Rivendare was the ruler of the city, a wealthy man who was dreadful enough in life and even worse in death. He delivered crates of plague-infested grain to one of the villages, thus having a direct hand in bringing about the Scourge. The tale of his son, Lord Aurius, is a true tragedy. Aurius was a paladin of the Silver Hand who lived his vows, even going so far as to assist in his monstrous father's demise. But strong as he was in his faith, it was not enough to save him from Rivendare's unnaturally savage blows. I'll say this for him: he held out till the end . . . but the end came. He became a death knight and took his father's dark place in that dark city.

The baron's cruelty extended even to a simple, faithful beast; he dragged his poor horse along with him into undeath. For years it was rumored that **Deathcharger** could be tamed by mortals, but I have never seen anyone living riding him.

Other artifacts sought by those who ventured into the city have been recovered and join those already present in Light's Hope Sanctum. One is the **Baron's Runeblade**—which, ironically, regenerates life force. His dagger **Bonescraper**—let's just say, it does what it says. The Baron's seal was also recovered. As much joy as traversing our lands gives me, there are always terrible reminders like these that darkness will have its way with human hearts.

I'LL HAVE YOU KNOW MY SKIN'S CRAWLING WITH GOOSEFLESH JUST READING THIS NAME.

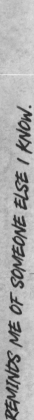

IX

Silvermoon City

YOU WON'T BELIEVE ME, BUT THIS PLACE IS BEAUTIFUL. REALLY. THANK YOU, MATHIAS. I'M GLAD TO HAVE SEEN IT.

The history of Quel'Thalas and the city of Silvermoon is messy, sad, and infuriating at times. The quel'dorei were once members of the Alliance, though initially only in a half-hearted manner. That changed when the orcs attacked during the Second War. And in the Third, the population was devastated by Arthas Menethil and the Scourge, who marched on the high elves' realm, slaughtered their king, Anasterian, and fouled the magical Sunwell from which the elves drew their power. I'm told only one out of ten elves survived. The quel'dorei renamed themselves "sin'dorei," which means "children of the blood," in honor of their fallen people. Far from being empathetic, the Grand Marshal of what remained of Lordaeron's forces treated the prince and his warriors with contempt and loathing, simply because they were quel'dorei. Finally, he sullied the name of the Alliance by forcing the blood elves to fight the Scourge on the most unforgiving front alone. His end was terrible, but better than he deserved. His bigotry cost the Alliance the sin'dorei who would ultimately cast their lot in with the Horde. In the end, with their addiction to first arcane magic and then fel energy, and the horrors brought to their doorstep and beyond by Arthas Menethil and the Scourge, the blood elves demonstrated great courage, determination, and strength. They are a fiercely proud people, and older injuries done to them are not forgotten.

REMINDS ME OF SOMEONE ELSE I KNOW.

The current leader of the blood elves, Regent Lord Lor'themar Theron, was once a commander of the elite group of rangers known as the Farstriders. Eventually he became second in command to Sylvanas, then named ranger lord of Silvermoon. He was among those who tried to stand against Arthas and saw firsthand the devastation of that attack. Lor'themar was a reliable leader as Regent Lord and a warden of the Sunwell when Prince Kael'thas was so long away. He has been an honorable enemy and a tentative ally I have fought beside. Although Lor'themar is, for the most part, a calm and steady individual, one must never forget he is also a master diplomat and a shrewd negotiator who always has the best interests of his people at heart. It is easy to underestimate him, but that would be a grievous mistake.

Armor Aside:
ARCANIST REGALIA

Despite their intricate stitching and elaborate collars, these vestments are far from delicate. The Arcanist Regalia is a symbol of accomplishment for highly practiced mages, each as formidable as the next.

Court of the Sun and the Bazaar

Much of the Court of the Sun survived the destruction of Arthas's assault, and here one can glimpse into the high elven glory of days past. The peak of its magnificence is Sunfury Spire, where once High King Anasterian Sunstrider ruled. Lor'themar now governs from here, in consultation with Grand Magister Rommath and Ranger-General Halduron Brightwing. In the grandeur of this place, one might be forgiven for momentarily forgetting the hardship Quel'Thalas has endured.

There are two sanctums in the city. One is located in the Bazaar area. I'm told a bright, deceptively pleasant clothing shop that once operated here concealed and ugly secret: the merchant—or should I say miscreant—utilized leper gnomes for labor. Turns out the merchant was a warlock, and he and his succubus were running the operation. There's a place in the southwest corner of the Bazaar, where the sin'dorei once gathered to debate and engage in largely friendly shouting matches. Our spies often attended to see who was sympathetic to the Alliance. I believe that tradition may be returning; during darker times, court priests could, quite literally, change the minds of those who protested against the leadership. A word of warning: Don't bother seeking out anyone in Murder Row. There is honor among spies, and precious little with thieves and cutthroats. Any friends we have in Silvermoon are much more important and higher up the ladder. Their names are never written down, not even here, out of respect for their positions.

REALLY? HOW EXCITING! IF YOU WERE INVOLVED, I DEMAND TO HEAR THE WHOLE STORY.

Isle of Quel'Danas

Also known as the "Sunwell Isle" and older than Silvermoon City itself, the Isle of Quel'Danas is the most sacred place in the world to the sin'dorei. Even in my lifetime, so much has happened to change the course of its history. Rising from the ground and reaching high into the sky is the Sunwell. Its arcane magic nourished the Highborne, enabling them to create Silvermoon and shape the forests of Quel'Thalas, thus bathing the Eversong Woods in eternal springtime. Arthas corrupted the Sunwell and, by extension, the elves themselves. Kael'thas was forced to destroy the ruined font of magic. Once addicted to its arcane magic, now the blood elves supplemented their need with fel energy. But thankfully the story doesn't end there. The draenei prophet Velen purified the Sunwell with the remaining spark of a naaru. As the Sunwell was polluted, destroyed, and eventually restored, so too have its people been.

Here also stands the Magisters' Terrace. It provides an excellent view of the harbor and the Sunwell Plateau, but it will forever be remembered as the place where Prince Kael'thas, the last of the Sunstrider line, finally fell. The site is cared for, but it has become almost a museum. And like a museum, it holds important pieces of history that help inform the present day.

I WANT A PHOENIX!

Tended to carefully are Kael'thas's own mount, a white hawkstrider, and a rare phoenix hatchling. It's still accurate to refer to it as such; phoenixes grow slowly. Extremely curious is the **Orb of the Sin'dorei:** a deceptively simple crystalline orb that grants its bearer the ability to look *exactly* like a blood elf. I would imagine its last owner was a demon, or perhaps a felblood elf, who utilized this while scurrying about Kael'thas's business. The **Quickening Blade of the Prince**, part of Kael'thas's collection, rests in a place of honor. Troubled as his reign and demise may have been, it seems the blood elves still carry grief for the wayward prince. It is a beautiful and mighty piece that almost seems to have a life of its own. It has not been cleaned of the blood it spilled.

THESE BLOOD ELVES, IT SEEMS, CONTINUE THE GHOULISH EASTERN KINGDOMS TRADITION. THEY'RE PRETTY MACABRE FOLK AS WELL.

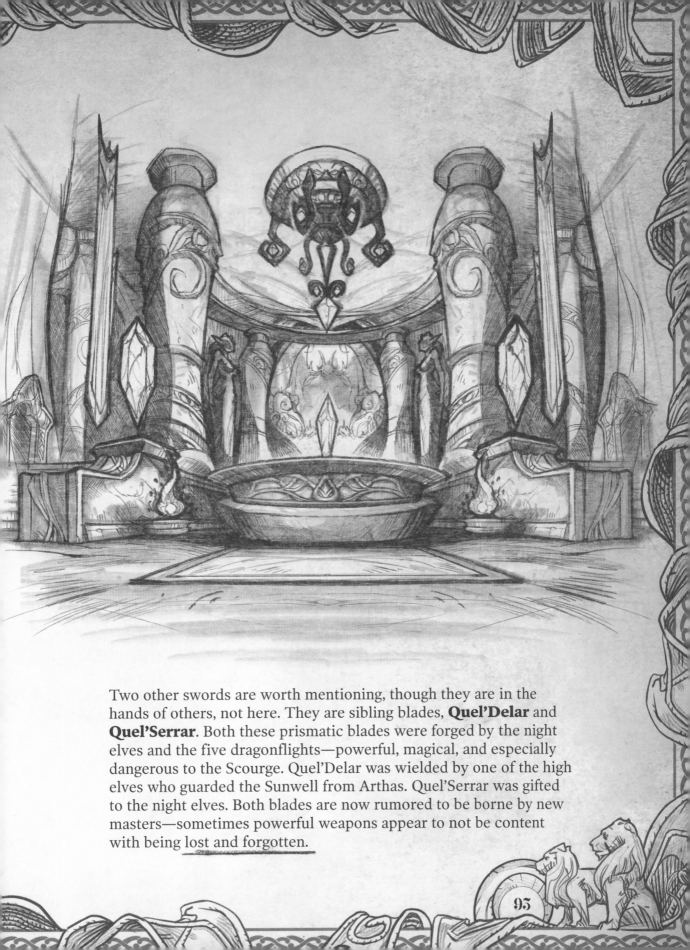

Two other swords are worth mentioning, though they are in the hands of others, not here. They are sibling blades, **Quel'Delar** and **Quel'Serrar**. Both these prismatic blades were forged by the night elves and the five dragonflights—powerful, magical, and especially dangerous to the Scourge. Quel'Delar was wielded by one of the high elves who guarded the Sunwell from Arthas. Quel'Serrar was gifted to the night elves. Both blades are now rumored to be borne by new masters—sometimes powerful weapons appear to not be content with being lost and forgotten.

Of course, the most famous weapon of the sin'dorei is **Felo'melorn**. It was carried by the late Anastarian for many centuries, an heirloom of the Sunstrider dynasty. It was a mighty blade, harnessing the power of fire, but it could not withstand the darkness of Frostmourne. Anastarian was lost that day, but his son recovered the pieces of Felo'melorn and had it reforged magically, stronger for the breaking. Kael'thas had it with him and was able to parry the sword that killed his father when he met Arthas in battle. It had been thought missing, gone with the elven prince, but recent rumors say it has been glimpsed in the hand of a true hero.

In the wake of the demon lord Kil'jaeden's defeat at the Sunwell, many powerful artifacts were discovered that may have been hoarded by the demon and his underlings. Some of these are heavily warded, which is a wise precaution—both to protect the innocents who watch over them and to deter those who would love to "liberate" them. Others have found their way into the safekeeping of the sin'dorei by different means; sometimes anonymous donations or offered for a limited exhibition. The mighty **Thori'dal, the Stars' Fury**, for instance, is a bow any archer would covet. One does not need to even carry a quiver; simply draw the bow and it magically conjures an arrow ready to be loosed. While the origins of this remarkable weapon remain unknown even to the sin'dorei, its power is clearly bound to the Sunwell. Through SI:7, the Alliance has been secretly negotiating for the return of the headdress of Alleria Windrunner and the now-tattered cape that belonged to Archmage Antonidas. We would like to see these personal items that belonged to fallen heroes given to those who loved them in life. ✱

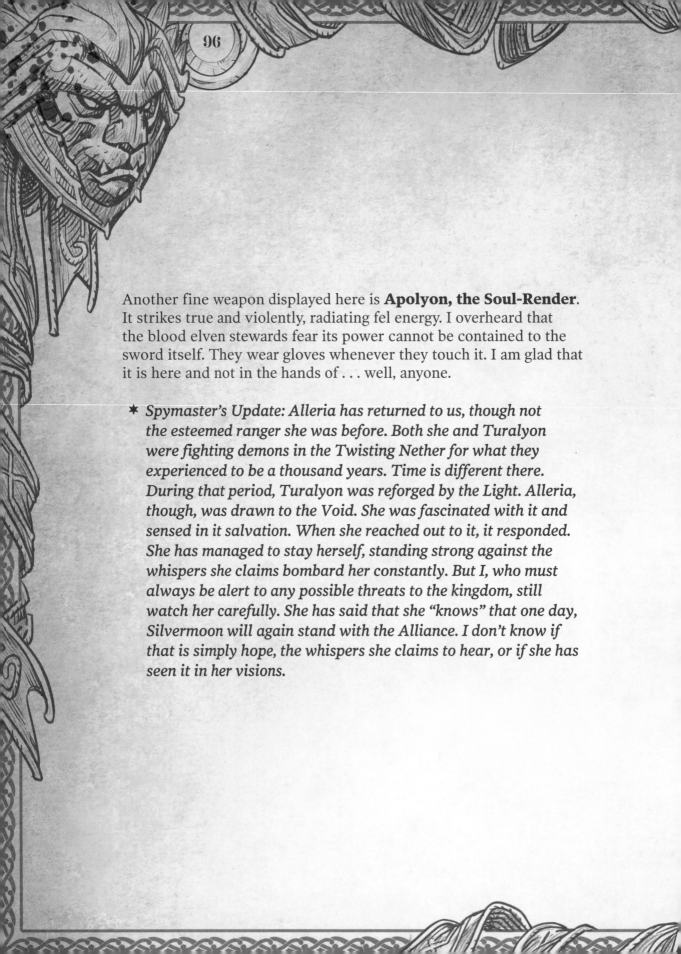

Another fine weapon displayed here is **Apolyon, the Soul-Render**. It strikes true and violently, radiating fel energy. I overheard that the blood elven stewards fear its power cannot be contained to the sword itself. They wear gloves whenever they touch it. I am glad that it is here and not in the hands of . . . well, anyone.

✴ *Spymaster's Update: Alleria has returned to us, though not the esteemed ranger she was before. Both she and Turalyon were fighting demons in the Twisting Nether for what they experienced to be a thousand years. Time is different there. During that period, Turalyon was reforged by the Light. Alleria, though, was drawn to the Void. She was fascinated with it and sensed in it salvation. When she reached out to it, it responded. She has managed to stay herself, standing strong against the whispers she claims bombard her constantly. But I, who must always be alert to any possible threats to the kingdom, still watch her carefully. She has said that she "knows" that one day, Silvermoon will again stand with the Alliance. I don't know if that is simply hope, the whispers she claims to hear, or if she has seen it in her visions.*

Armor Aside:
GIANTSTALKER ARMOR

Gear as imposing as its name, the Giantstalker armor worn by skilled hunters provides both protection and intimidation. Some proficient users even claim that their pets perform better while the garb is donned, showing greater tenacity in battle.

X
Hillsbrad Foothills and Silverpine Forest

The Hillsbrad Foothills are troubled lands, rife with monsters: Scourge, worgen, ghosts, and the worst kind of monsters—humans. Durnholde Keep was once under the command of Lieutenant General Lord Aedelas Blackmoore. From that base, he oversaw all the orcish internment camps that were created after the Second War. Upon discovery of an orphan orc child, Blackmoore, son of a traitor, plotted treason himself. He raised the child to be a gladiator who would be fiercely loyal to him. The idea was that this gladiator would lead an army of orcs against the Alliance with Blackmoore at their head. Of course, almost everyone in Azeroth knows who that orc was.

Blackmoore was a murderous, angry drunk who relished bullying those who could not fight back. I am of course firmly for Stormwind and the Alliance, but I am glad that Thrall, an orc who believes in the possibility of peace, still lives, and the treacherous Aedelas is rotting in the rubble of his brutal keep.

Refugees from Stormwind came to this area after the First War, fleeing a city overrun by orcs. The people of the small coastal town of Southshore welcomed them. But nothing good lasts, it seems. Years later, Forsaken assaulted the place, and it was overrun with blight.✲

IT WAS SAURFANG, WASN'T IT? OR WAS IT ETRIGG? GARONA, MAYBE?

OH! IT'S THRALL, IS IT? GOOD ON YOU, YOU GREAT GREEN BLOKE.

✲ *Spymaster's Update: Before the close of the Fourth War, the Alliance was finally able to reclaim the ruins of Southshore and is still working on driving out the remaining threats. Hopefully this does not affect the armistice—or the work that Calia and Lilian are doing.*

Silverpine and Shadowfang Keep

While the smell of pine needles invigorates my mind and sense of wanderlust, Silverpine is no more cheerful than Hillsbrad Foothills. In the south, Greymane's now-breached wall still stands. We are glad of our worgen allies and the Greymane family, but the city remains as isolated as ever. Centuries ago, the worgen, cursed night elf druids, were banished to the Emerald Dream. Unfortunately, one Archmage Arugal, in a misguided attempt to help Gilneas fight the Scourge, summoned them back to Azeroth. The ferocious worgen did take care of the Scourge but also turned on any humans they could find, namely, the Gilnean people. Worgen breached the defenses of the local baron, Silverlaine, killing him and his family. Poor bastard still haunts the place, they say. Arugal was driven mad with guilt, named the place Shadowfang Keep, and retreated there with his worgen "children." After his death at the hands of the Horde, the Lich King saw fit to bring him back as one of his puppets. After *that*, Arugal was, finally, put to a true end. May he be miserable in the afterlife, whatever that may be.

Shadowfang Keep had a new master for a time: another traitor to the Gilnean crown, Lord Vincent Godfrey of Gilneas. He threw himself from a cliff rather than accept a worgen as his king and was raised by a bloody Val'kyr. He wielded, and presumably named, the **Staff of Isolation**, killing many in his wake. A lonely and unhappy man, it seems, but I for one won't weep for him. He's dead now, too. Let's hope he stays that way.

Our contact at Shadowfang Keep is Ivar Bloodfang, leader of the Bloodfang pack, and they have claimed Fenris Isle as their own. Their hatred of the undead is endless. Agents should be careful when making contact, for while they are still our allies, they are very close to feral. Ivar prowled Shadowfang many times in search of Godfrey and has rescued several valuable and historic items that are now stored in Fenris Keep. I cannot think of better protectors of such items than the Bloodfangs.

THIS "BECOMING UNDEAD" TENDENCY SEEMS LIKE QUITE THE PROBLEM. CAN'T YOU DO ANYTHING ABOUT IT?

Among the most interesting are Baron Silverlaine's family seal and a locket. The locket has stayed closed; no one appears interested in what or who the ill-fated Baron treasured. A huge sword has also been recovered—**Shadowfang** has the bite of a wolf and shadowy powers that suit a weapon named for such a place. And displayed carefully is a dagger made of meteorite, a stone gifted from the sky.

On a lighter note, multiple individuals claim to have discovered—and are wearing—the robes of Arugal, which is of course impossible.

Armor Aside:

CENARION RAIMENT

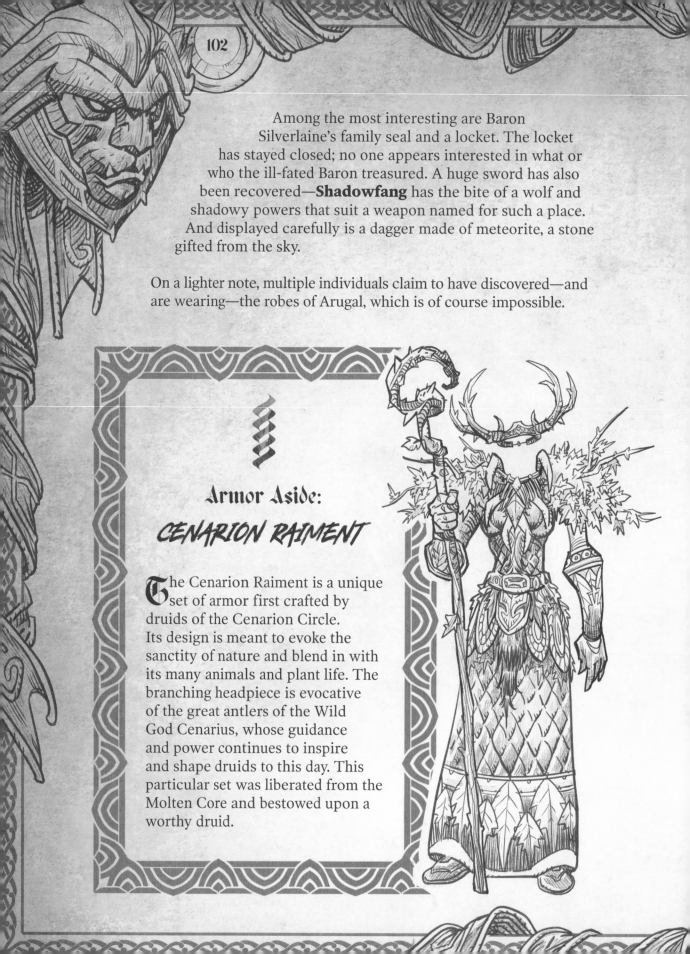

The Cenarion Raiment is a unique set of armor first crafted by druids of the Cenarion Circle. Its design is meant to evoke the sanctity of nature and blend in with its many animals and plant life. The branching headpiece is evocative of the great antlers of the Wild God Cenarius, whose guidance and power continues to inspire and shape druids to this day. This particular set was liberated from the Molten Core and bestowed upon a worthy druid.

I'M SHOCKED—SHOCKED, I TELL YOU—TO LEARN THIS.

Tol Barad

This entire peninsula is one I would just as soon not have to visit on a regular basis, but certain things must have eyes kept upon them. One of the largest known cemeteries in Azeroth is here, and not all of its occupants are safely sleeping in the earth. Elsewhere, one must navigate a sea of creatures: giant spiders and their webs, every conceivable variety of undead.

Once, there was a semblance of order, when the Kirin Tor was able to contain a prison called Baradin Hold full of monstrous creatures, including demons. One of the worst of the inmates, a demon called Occu'thar, broke free of its cell and devoured all of its fellow prisoners in the west wing. Unfortunately for him, such gluttony rendered him too large to escape. The creature literally had eyes everywhere; it could conjure them at will. Eventually it was killed, but many others remained—until there was a breakout. Most were slain by hired swords, but some escaped. Our latest intel says that some of them are still in the prison . . . but there's no warden at the prison any longer. What's left of that job is held by Baradin's Wardens, founded and led by Duke Reginald Baradin II. Since that good man's death, the officer in charge now is Commander Marcus Johnson, who confirmed that our intelligence is accurate. There's that at least—bad news, but correct news. He tells me that now and then, some of them come out, but never in force. They're killed on sight, but we don't know how many of them there are. Johnson looks as grim as a grave when he delivers that disturbing bit of information. All they know is what little was jotted down in a notebook by one of the Kirin Tor mages, found beside his skeleton:

CAN'T MAKE IT TO RETREAT POINT, TOO MANY DEMONS. MY LAST STAND IS HERE. IF ANYONE FINDS THIS, TELL THE KIRIN TOR THAT I TOOK AS MANY OF THEM WITH ME AS I COULD.

On a less horrible note, the camp's quartermaster, Alaric Brazie, has developed a fondness for the wildlife, especially gulls and the local fox, which is almost extinct. He rescues abandoned litters and injured birds, always trying to find homes for them. I think he has better luck with the fox kits than the gulls.

I WANT A FOX KIT!

The nearby village of Rustberg was home to many of those who staffed the Baradin Hold. When they were recalled after the uprising, the vacancy was filled by unscrupulous persons, namely, pirates. Human, tauren, orc, gnome . . . how odd that the races mostly come together only for nefarious purposes. Still, like Booty Bay, it's a fine place to get the latest rumors. Our current contact there is Jamison Gray,* first mate of the ship Bloody Dawn. His information is accurate, but I fear he will one day say too much while in his cups.

I WOULD NEVER DO THIS. NEVER.

I TAKE UMBRAGE AT THIS.

* *Spymaster's Update: Unfortunately, Gray was indeed discovered and killed. Brazie now serves in his stead, in a way; some of the fox kits and gulls bear messages from him that are borne to me by trusted adventurers. I still need to find someone in Rustberg, though; pirates travel, and learn more, than a quartermaster.*

I COULD HAVE A GO WITH THEM IF
YOU LIKE. I HAVE THE SORT OF FACE
PEOPLE JUST NATURALLY TRUST.

⚡ XI ⚡
Tirisfal Glades

ormerly a part of the kingdom of Lordaeron, Tirisfal Glades was once green, fertile farmland. Now the entire area has a pall over it.✱ It was one of the first areas to fall to the plague of undeath and now belongs to the Forsaken.

The Balnir Farmstead, among others, was known for breeding the great white horses of Lordaeron. King Anduin's horse Reverence comes from this stock, and His Majesty honors the tradition of paladins and priests by naming his horse for a quality he admires. Near the Balnir farm is the grave of Invincible, who was the beloved steed of Arthas. So distraught was the young prince over Invincible's death that he buried the horse and placed a plaque to commemorate him:

> INVINCIBLE: BELOVED STEED OF PRINCE ARTHAS MENETHIL. LOYAL AND GREAT OF HEART, MAY YOU FIND PEACE IN DEATH. PURE STREAMS AND GREEN PASTURES, DEVOTED FRIEND.

Cruelly, Arthas and his twisted ways did not let Invincible find peace in death. He raised the noble beast to once again serve him as an undead creature.

OH FOR TIDES' SAKE. I GIVE UP. SOD YOU, ARTHAS. YOU BLOODY MONSTER.

The Scarlet Crusade, or members of the Scarlet Crusade, inhabited this area as well, putting themselves in a Forsaken-rich environment to kill as many of the undead as possible. They were a cult as cruel and narrow-minded as they come. The Scarlet Crusade spread everywhere at once, it seemed: in a bastion of Stratholme, in Hearthglen, in the town of Tyr's Hand, and, most unforgettably, holed up in a once-sacred place they renamed the Scarlet Monastery.

I GENUINELY WAS NOT EXPECTING TO HEAR THAT. USUALLY I LIKE BLOKES WHO ARE KIND TO ANIMALS. SURELY THERE MUST HAVE BEEN SOME GOOD IN HIM, THEN?

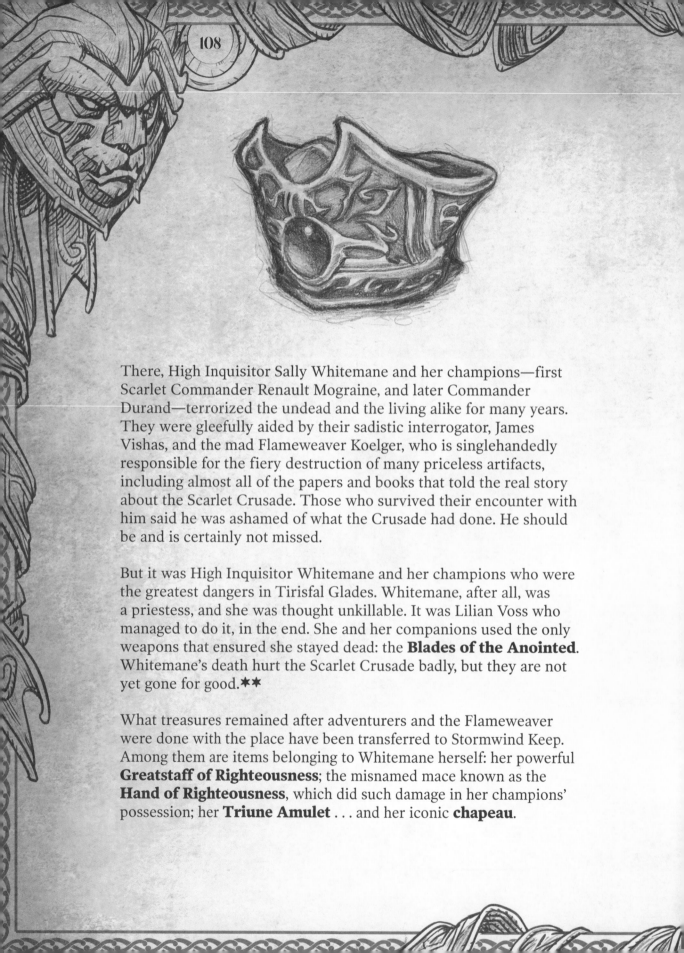

There, High Inquisitor Sally Whitemane and her champions—first Scarlet Commander Renault Mograine, and later Commander Durand—terrorized the undead and the living alike for many years. They were gleefully aided by their sadistic interrogator, James Vishas, and the mad Flameweaver Koelger, who is singlehandedly responsible for the fiery destruction of many priceless artifacts, including almost all of the papers and books that told the real story about the Scarlet Crusade. Those who survived their encounter with him said he was ashamed of what the Crusade had done. He should be and is certainly not missed.

But it was High Inquisitor Whitemane and her champions who were the greatest dangers in Tirisfal Glades. Whitemane, after all, was a priestess, and she was thought unkillable. It was Lilian Voss who managed to do it, in the end. She and her companions used the only weapons that ensured she stayed dead: the **Blades of the Anointed**. Whitemane's death hurt the Scarlet Crusade badly, but they are not yet gone for good.✶✶

What treasures remained after adventurers and the Flameweaver were done with the place have been transferred to Stormwind Keep. Among them are items belonging to Whitemane herself: her powerful **Greatstaff of Righteousness**; the misnamed mace known as the **Hand of Righteousness**, which did such damage in her champions' possession; her **Triune Amulet** . . . and her iconic **chapeau**.

★ *Spymaster's Update #1: It is with sadness, but not regret, that I report the Alliance has recently inflicted its own massive wound upon this land. It was necessary to bring the troops and equipment needed for the Battle of Lordaeron. Our king is always reluctant to resort to violence, but he was well aware that Sylvanas needed to be held accountable for the slaughter of so many at Teldrassil. So much heavy weaponry, horses, and people necessitated felling trees and churning up the soil. The war begun there is over, but as always, the scars remain. I hope that with time, unlike Dead Scar in the green grass of Eversong Woods, this scar will recover. One day, we will learn how to clear the plague from this area and will again see green grass and waving trees. Or so I like to tell myself.*

★★ *Spymaster's Update #2: I have been informed that, to the best of our knowledge, the Scarlet Crusade has been eliminated entirely. It seems that only the undead could truly destroy those who had tormented them for so long. The honor belonged to the Ebon Blade, who came to the Monastery to stamp out the Crusade for good . . . and raise the corpse of its most recognizable member, Whitemane, to become one of their Four Horsemen. Thankfully, the Scarlet Crusade's influence has dwindled in recent years. However, rats and roaches have a way of surviving, as is evidenced by a group dubbing itself the "Scarlet Brotherhood," whose only attacks come from anonymous pamphlets spouting absurdities. As for Whitemane, what an ironic twist of fate that she who so despised the undead has become one of them. There is some grotesque poetry in it.*

I SAW ONE OF THOSE! THEIR THEORIES CAN GET A BIT RACY, CAN'T THEY?

XII

The Undercity

Like many of us who lived through Arthas's rampage, I had friends in Lordaeron. Some became Forsaken. Some remain Scourge. All are dead now.

Rather than dwell in the city proper, the Forsaken chose to make their capital below it. Repurposing the crypts and catacombs for everyday use makes sense, as the Undercity is much more defensible than the city above it. I would venture to guess it was also to emphasize that they are no longer the living people they were before Arthas came.

Below ground are the putrid green sewers and indeed an undercity. It is, as you can imagine, difficult to get spies inside unnoticed. As fate would have it, SI:7 has a little green card up its sleeve. Renzik "the Shiv",✶✶ our goblin eyes and rather large ears in Horde territory, returned after one trip with sketches of the labyrinthine city, including the Royal Quarter. Sylvanas once held court here, first with the demon Varimathras, later with Nathanos to stand at her right hand. Recently, she ascended to warchief of the Horde.✶✶✶

A semblance—more a mockery—of normal "life" goes on here. There is a bank, an auction house, vendors that specialize in poisons and potions—and in one case, pet cockroaches. Warriors train with their weapons. I think the worst part of this place, however—and that's saying something—is the monstrous Apothecarium. It is a veritable chamber of horrors: dissection, vivisection, and torture, all approved by Sylvanas herself in search of developing better and more lethal poisons, blight, and other toxins. Master Apothecary Faranell was once a respected, if overly curious, alchemist in Dalaran. He enjoyed experimenting with different brews and tinctures, trying this or that to cure something or improve one's health. He has now been twisted by death into a sadist and keeps humans in this place for torture and experimentation. Once we did

I LIKE MY FINGERS AND TOES RIGHT WHERE THEY ARE. THANK YOU VERY MUCH. I'LL HOLD YOUR CAPE. WAIT FOR YOU OUTSIDE. FLYNN FAIRWIND'S GOOD OUT HERE.

get the upper hand on him. Faranell had in his possession a journal written by another apothecary named Berard. From Berard's notes, Faranell was able to create a new plague. "Blight," it was called. Putress released this new plague at the Wrathgate, killing Alliance and Horde alike. An SI:7 agent has since recovered that notebook. While it comes too late to stop the blight, it gives us an invaluable insight into what went into Faranell's first one. Perhaps we can create something to fight against the inevitable next incarnation.✱

There is an **Orb of Translocation** here in the outer courtyard that transports one to Silvermoon City. If its elegance looks out of place amid the ruins, it is because it was a gift from the blood elves. I always remind myself of it in case of emergency; I can at least attempt to negotiate with blood elves, but the abominations that lumber about as guards of the Undercity understand no such niceties.

A poorly kept secret is that the best way for Alliance to enter the Undercity is through the sewers. But once before, and only once, I snuck in through the main entrance. It is nothing I would care to experience ever again. In a very disturbing way, it feels as if Arthas just left. Faint echoes of the broken bell toll barely at the edge of hearing, so like our own comforting cathedral bell, and yet so changed. And in the throne room, old, crusted blood still discolors the seal of Lordaeron on the floor. If you stand perfectly still, you'd almost swear you can make out the echoes of father and son sharing their final words before Terenas was slain. Be it ghosts or the horrible memory this place holds, lingering is ill advised.

BY THE TIDES, THAT SOUND WOULD TERRIFY ME. LUCKILY THERE'S THAT SEWER OPTION!

115

IF WE'RE BEING HONEST, WHICH I AM, THIS IS THE NICEST OF THE THREE EPITAPHS. I SEE HE LIKED THE LINE ABOUT A BLOODY CROWN SO MUCH HE QUOTED IT IN HIS OWN TOMB-SIDE READING MATERIAL.

WENT BACK AND CHECKED. NOT "BLOODY CROWN." "CROWN INCARNADINE." I GUESS HE FELT GOOD ABOUT WHERE HE WAS GOING IN THE AFTERLIFE. YOU SEEM TO HAVE A DISTRESSING NUMBER OF MURDERED KINGS AND STAINED CROWNS STREWN ABOUT, MATHIAS.

It's not uncommon for tombs to be carved long before the occupant's death. Such is the case with Terenas; the words on the plaque were carved by two different hands. The first part simply states: "Here lies King Terenas Menethil II." Of course, it's not true. Arthas stole his father's urn and scattered the meaningless ashes to the wind before they could be interred here, using the urn to house the remains of the lich Kel'Thuzad. The tomb is completely empty. The second part, clearly written after Terenas's brutal death, reads:

LAST TRUE KING OF LORDAERON. GREAT WERE HIS DEEDS, LONG WAS HIS REIGN, UNTHINKABLE WAS HIS DEATH. MAY THE FATHER LIE BLAMELESS FOR THE DEEDS OF THE SON. MAY THE BLOODIED CROWN STAY LOST AND FORGOTTEN.

While we're not sure who added the second part, SI:7 believes it to have been done on the order of King Thoras Trollbane, who was once a great friend to Terenas.

* *Spymaster's Update #1: At the Battle for Lordaeron, Sylvanas exceeded even my expectations: as we feared, there was an improved formula of the deadly blight. It now clouds over the Undercity and the ruins of Lordaeron. She released the blight not only on her enemies but on her own people. Currently the Undercity is rendered uninhabitable, not just for the living but the dead, too.*

** *Spymaster's Update #2: Renzik has reported that parts of the upper area, the ruins of old Lordaeron, appear slightly less dangerous, as if the blight is slowly fading. One can venture there, but one must be quick about it. The toxic blight will likely take a very long time to disperse completely.*

*** *Spymaster's Update #3: Continuing the trend of her appalling disregard for life, Sylvanas has abandoned the Horde and killed High Overlord Saurfang. Whatever path she now walks is beyond us.*

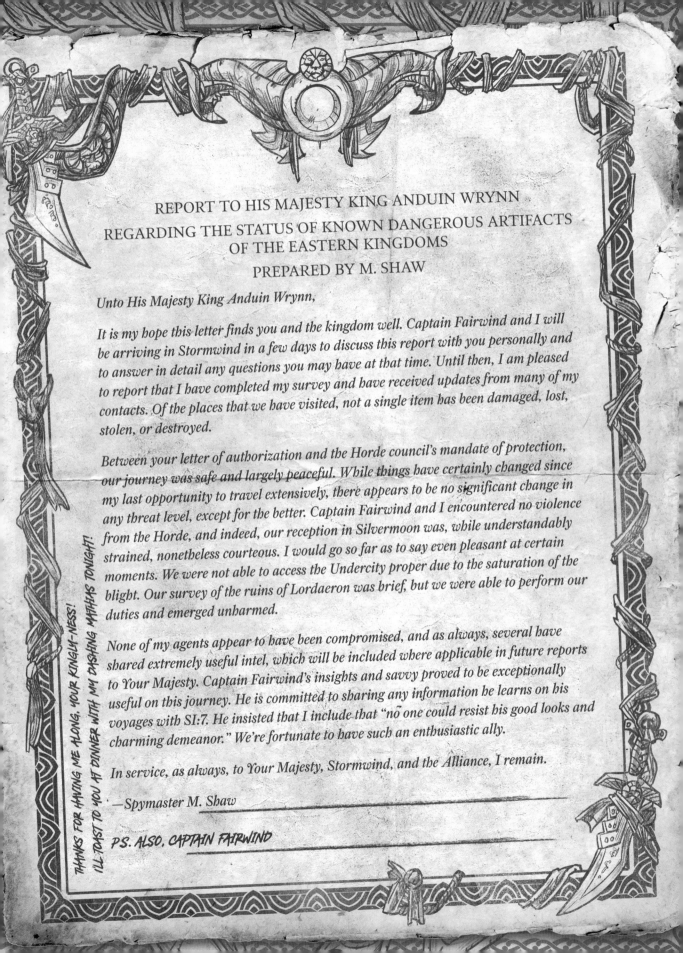

REPORT TO HIS MAJESTY KING ANDUIN WRYNN
REGARDING THE STATUS OF KNOWN DANGEROUS ARTIFACTS OF THE EASTERN KINGDOMS
PREPARED BY M. SHAW

Unto His Majesty King Anduin Wrynn,

It is my hope this letter finds you and the kingdom well. Captain Fairwind and I will be arriving in Stormwind in a few days to discuss this report with you personally and to answer in detail any questions you may have at that time. Until then, I am pleased to report that I have completed my survey and have received updates from many of my contacts. Of the places that we have visited, not a single item has been damaged, lost, stolen, or destroyed.

Between your letter of authorization and the Horde council's mandate of protection, our journey was safe and largely peaceful. While things have certainly changed since my last opportunity to travel extensively, there appears to be no significant change in any threat level, except for the better. Captain Fairwind and I encountered no violence from the Horde, and indeed, our reception in Silvermoon was, while understandably strained, nonetheless courteous. I would go so far as to say even pleasant at certain moments. We were not able to access the Undercity proper due to the saturation of the blight. Our survey of the ruins of Lordaeron was brief, but we were able to perform our duties and emerged unharmed.

None of my agents appear to have been compromised, and as always, several have shared extremely useful intel, which will be included where applicable in future reports to Your Majesty. Captain Fairwind's insights and savvy proved to be exceptionally useful on this journey. He is committed to sharing any information he learns on his voyages with SI:7. He insisted that I include that "no one could resist his good looks and charming demeanor." We're fortunate to have such an enthusiastic ally.

In service, as always, to Your Majesty, Stormwind, and the Alliance, I remain.

—Spymaster M. Shaw

P.S. ALSO, CAPTAIN FAIRWIND

THANKS FOR HAVING ME ALONG. YOUR KINGLY-NESS!
I'LL TOAST TO YOU AT DINNER WITH MY DASHING MATHIAS TONIGHT!

FLYNN FAIRWIND'S OFFICIAL EXPLORING NOTES!

STORMWIND: CROWNED, MURDERED . . . A TOMBSTONE BY A LIGHTHOUSE. FOLKS FROM STORMWIND CAME FROM LORDAERON ORIGINALLY. RIGHT?

JANEIRO'S POINT: TARNISHED CROWN

STROMGARDE KEEP: KING TERENAS MENETHIL II. HE WAS KING OF LORDAERON. WASN'T THERE SOMETHING CRYPTIC ABOUT HIS CROWN?

THAT EPITAPH ON KING THORAS'S GRAVE: PREPARE TO BURY IT . . . KEEP THE SECRET . . . DO NOT AN ISLAND BE. HE AND TERENAS WERE FRIENDS. DID THEY MEAN SOMETHING TO BE BURIED ON AN ISLAND?

SILVERMOON: LOST AND FORGOTTEN . . . THAT'S GOT ME THINKING. LOST AND FORGOTTEN . . .

TIRISFAL GLADES: GROTESQUE POETRY . . . LIKE THOSE EPITAPHS WE KEEP SEEING ALL OVER THE PLACE. I FEEL LIKE THERE'S SOMETHING THERE. SOME BURIED SOMETHING JUST WAITING TO BE UNCOVERED!

UNDERCITY: BLOOD STILL CRUSTED ON THE GROUND . . . "MAY THE BLOODIED CROWN STAY LOST AND FORGOTTEN."

ONE LESS-THAN-OFFICIAL REPORT FROM THE GREAT CAPTAIN FLYNN FAIRWIND TO THE DEVILISHLY HANDSOME AND CAPABLE SPYMASTER MATHIAS SHAW:

I DIDN'T THINK I'D BE ANY GOOD AT THIS SPY BUSINESS. GOING AROUND THE WORLD, LEARNING NEW THINGS, EXPLORING, ALL DANDY AT THAT. AND YET, HERE I GO, SORTING OUT THE SADDEST PUZZLE I'VE EVER SEEN. I'M WRITING THIS DOWN MOSTLY SO YOU REMEMBER FOR YOUR SPY-BOOKKEEPING. I'M SURE THAT'S A THING YOU DO ANYWAY.

FINDING ALL THESE NUGGETS OF INFORMATION GOT MY MIND SPINNING ABOUT BURIED TREASURE OF SOME LONG DEAD KINGS. INSTEAD . . . I KNOW WHERE THE BLOODIED CROWN OF KING TERENAS MENETHIL II IS. YOU AND I FOUND IT, TO MAKE SURE, AND BURIED IT BACK AS IT WAS IN THAT LITTLE UNATTENDED GRAVE ON THE LIGHTHOUSE IN STORMWIND HARBOR. WITH THE KING OF LORDAERON DEAD, HIS BODY DESTROYED, AND HIS GRAVE IMPOSSIBLE TO REACH FOR MOURNING, THE REFUGEES OF LORDAERON MUST HAVE WANTED A WAY TO HONOR THEIR FALLEN KING. THIS WAS THEIR QUIET, REVERENT WAY OF DOING SO. I'VE SALUTED MANY FRIENDS LOST AT SEA: MAYBE THEY NEEDED A PLACE TO DO THE SAME? EITHER WAY, THE LOCATION STAYS BETWEEN YOU AND ME, JUST LIKE TERENAS WANTED. LIPS SEALED LIKE A VAULT. CROSS MY HEART. THANK YOU FOR GOING BACK OUT TO THAT ISLAND WITH ME TO CHECK MY HAREBRAINED THEORY . . . I THINK IN DOING SO, WE HONORED SOME FOLKS WHO LOST EVERYTHING.

SIGNING OFF,
CAPTAIN FLYNN FAIRWIND

XOXO

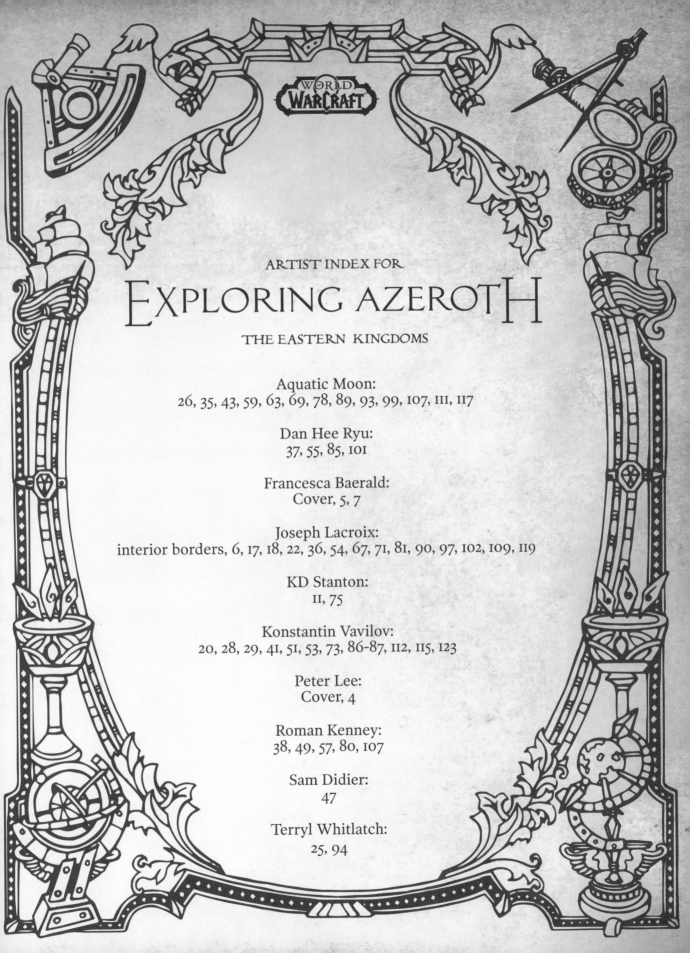

ARTIST INDEX FOR

EXPLORING AZEROTH

THE EASTERN KINGDOMS

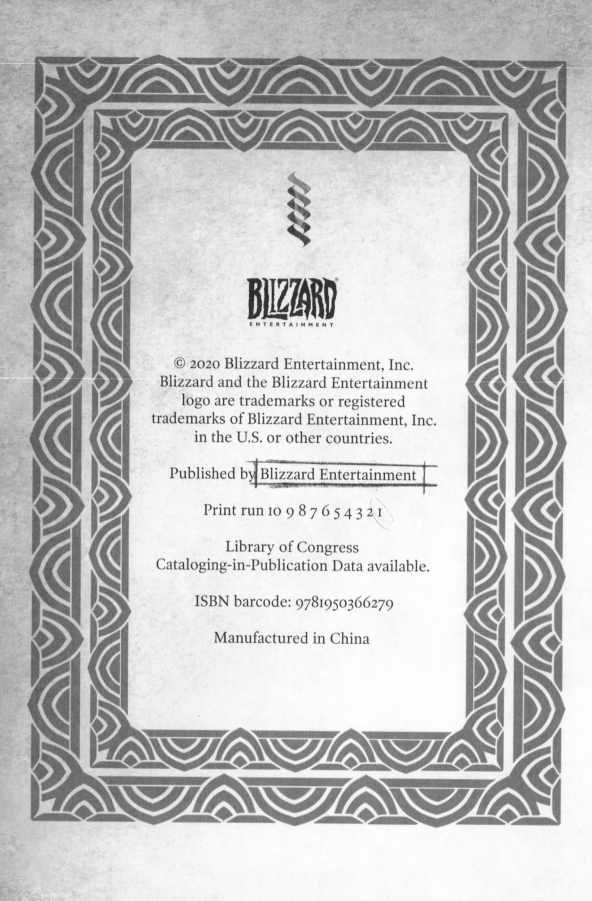

Published by Blizzard Entertainment

Print run 10 9 8 7 6 5 4 3 2 1

Library of Congress
Cataloging-in-Publication Data available.

ISBN barcode: 9781950366279

Manufactured in China

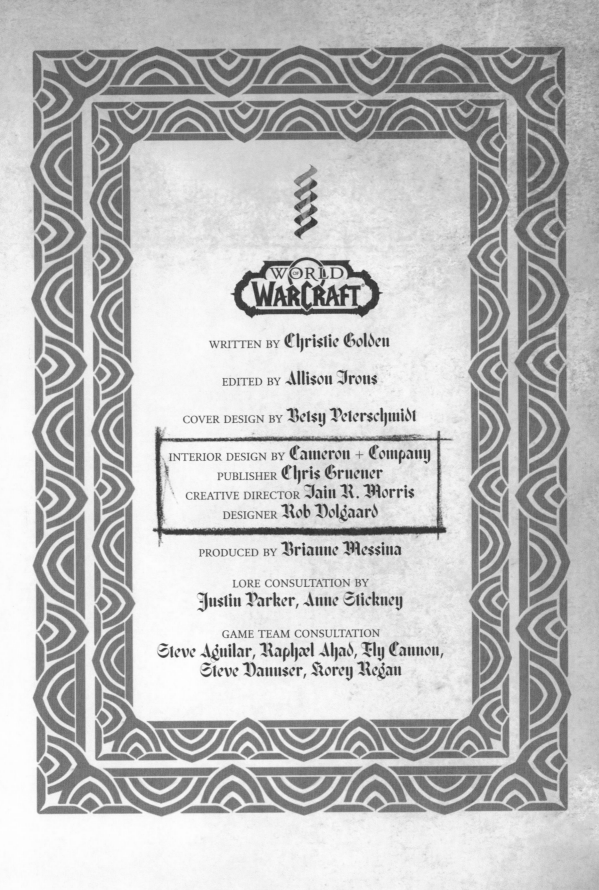

WORLD of WARCRAFT

WRITTEN BY **Christie Golden**

EDITED BY **Allison Irons**

COVER DESIGN BY **Betsy Peterschmidt**

INTERIOR DESIGN BY **Cameron + Company**
PUBLISHER **Chris Gruener**
CREATIVE DIRECTOR **Iain R. Morris**
DESIGNER **Rob Volgaard**

PRODUCED BY **Brianne Messina**

LORE CONSULTATION BY
Justin Parker, Anne Stickney

GAME TEAM CONSULTATION
**Steve Aguilar, Raphael Ahad, Ely Cannon,
Steve Danuser, Korey Regan**

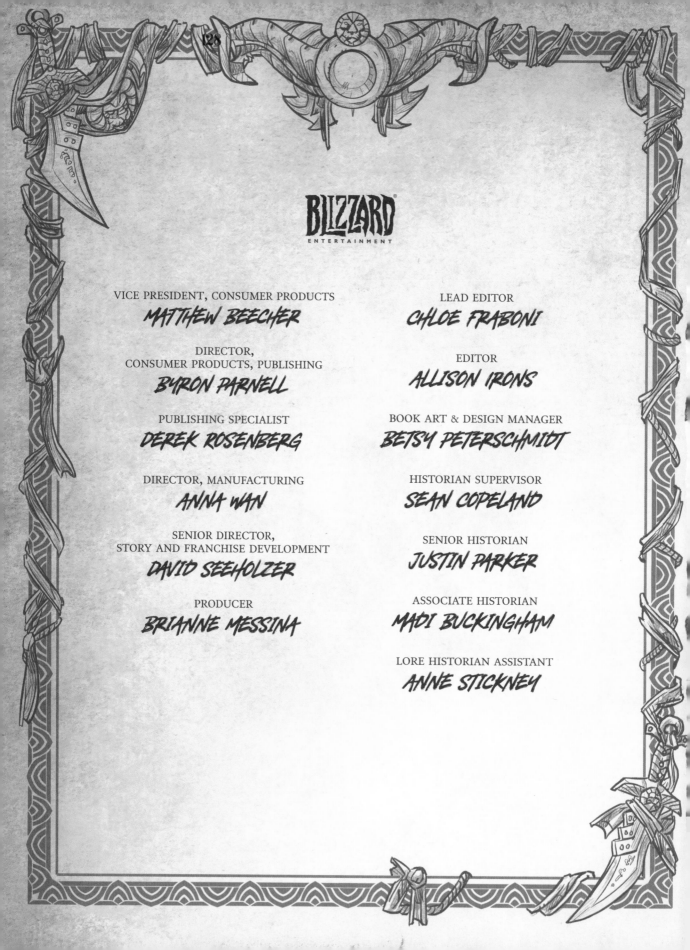

BLIZZARD
ENTERTAINMENT

VICE PRESIDENT, CONSUMER PRODUCTS
MATTHEW BEECHER

DIRECTOR,
CONSUMER PRODUCTS, PUBLISHING
BYRON PARNELL

PUBLISHING SPECIALIST
DEREK ROSENBERG

DIRECTOR, MANUFACTURING
ANNA WAN

SENIOR DIRECTOR,
STORY AND FRANCHISE DEVELOPMENT
DAVID SEEHOLZER

PRODUCER
BRIANNE MESSINA

LEAD EDITOR
CHLOE FRABONI

EDITOR
ALLISON IRONS

BOOK ART & DESIGN MANAGER
BETSY PETERSCHMIDT

HISTORIAN SUPERVISOR
SEAN COPELAND

SENIOR HISTORIAN
JUSTIN PARKER

ASSOCIATE HISTORIAN
MADI BUCKINGHAM

LORE HISTORIAN ASSISTANT
ANNE STICKNEY